Til There Was You

A Misfit Inn Novella

Kait Nolan

Til There Was You

Written and published by Kait Nolan

Copyright 2020 Kait Nolan

Cover design by Kait Nolan

All rights reserved, including the right to reproduce this book, or portions thereof, in any form.

AUTHOR'S NOTE: The following is a work of fiction. All people, places, and events are purely products of the author's imagination. Any resemblance to actual people, places, or events is entirely coincidental.

NO AI TRAINING: Without in any way limiting the author's exclusive rights under copyright, any use of this publication to "train" generative artificial intelligence (AI) technologies to generate text is expressly prohibited. The author reserves all rights to license uses of this work for generative AI training and development of machine learning language models.

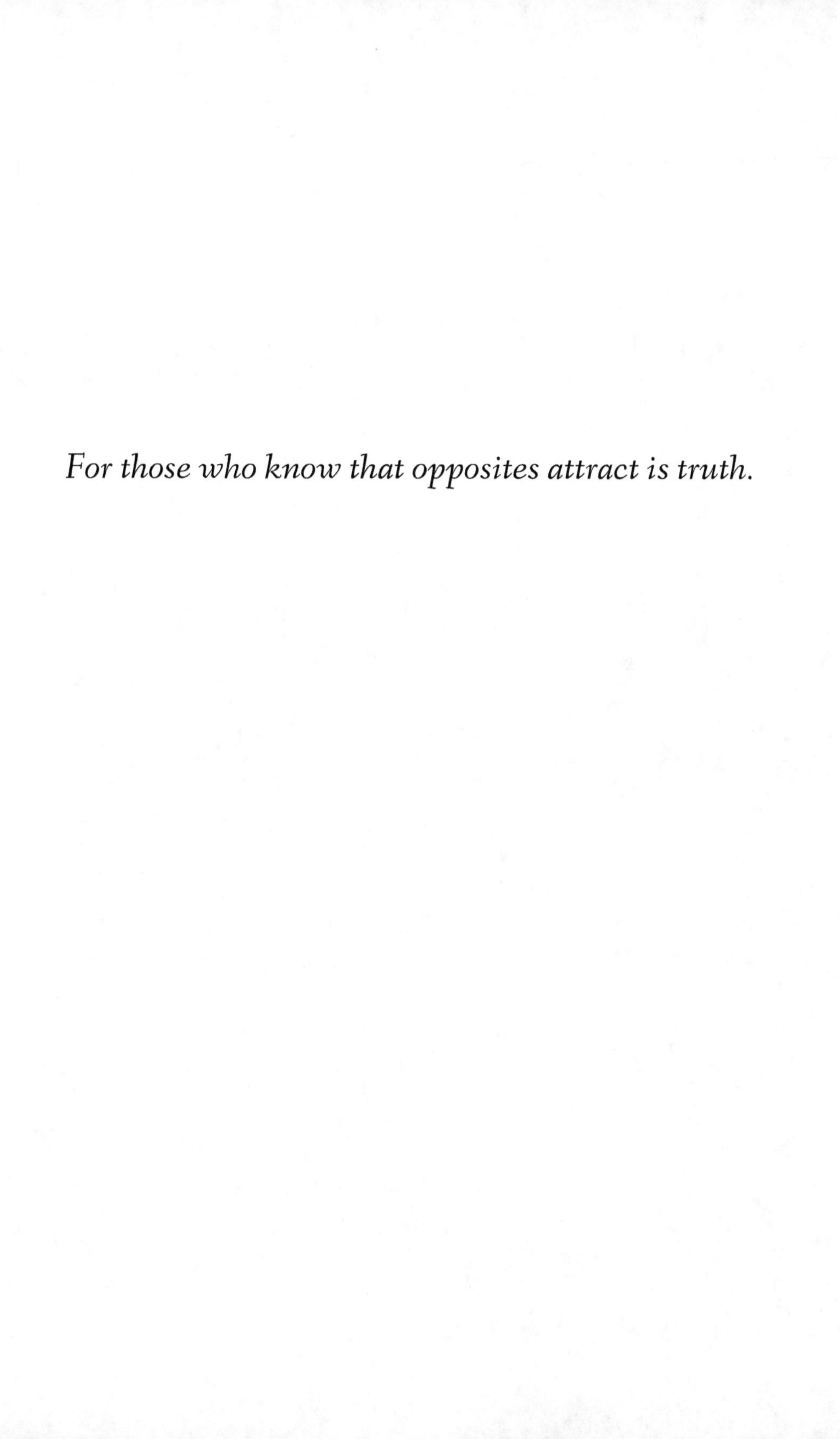

For those who know that opposites attract is truth.

A Letter to Readers

Dear Reader,

A few points of note:

A shorter version of this story was originally published as *Once Upon A Wedding,* part of my Meet Cute Romance series. I have expanded it by more than 50% and turned it into a full novella. As such, the original version has been removed from sale.

This book is set in the Deep South. As such, it contains a great deal of colorful, colloquial, and occasionally grammatically incorrect language. This is a deliberate choice on my part as an author to most accurately represent the region where I have lived my entire life. This book also contains swearing and pre-marital sex between the lead couple, as those things are part of the realistic lives of characters of this generation, and of many of my readers.

If any of these things are not your cup of tea, please consider that you may not be the right audience for this book. There are scores of other books out there that are written with you in mind. In fact, I've got a list of some of my favorite authors who write on the sweeter side on my website at https://kaitnolan.com/on-the-sweeter-side/

If you choose to stick with me, I hope you enjoy!

Happy reading!

Kait

Chapter One

"I can't believe I let you talk me into this insanity." Cayla Black bitched into her white wine spritzer. Denver knew it was the only drink the active, single mom ever ordered, and she was looking at it like she wished it were something stronger.

"Are you backing out?" Kennedy Reynolds' voice held a rare note of panic. His best bartender wasn't prone to panic, and Denver paused in the noisy task of racking glassware before the dinner rush to listen in more closely.

"Oh, I can do it. I didn't say I couldn't do it," Cayla insisted, as though the suggestion that she couldn't mocked her event planner pride. "You just need to be fully aware that your race to the altar is giving me wrinkles. You see this line right here?" She pointed to some nonexistent blemish on her forehead. "I got that convincing Jolene Lowrey to make her prize-winning red velvet cake for your wedding. You're just lucky she has as much fondness for Xander's extremely fine backside as you do."

Kennedy snickered and wiped down the already clean bar. "Your sacrifice is duly noted, but I object to 'race to the altar'. We've been waiting for years. We just didn't know we were waiting."

"Oh, that's...sort of lovely." Cayla's face went soft for a moment, then her brows came back down. "Do not get me sidetracked," she warned, flipping open the bulging planner at her elbow.

Not for the first time since Kennedy had announced her engagement to Xander Kincaid—interim sheriff of Stone County—Denver wondered if there was a bun in the oven. He'd heard the pair had been hot and heavy in high school, but Kennedy had taken off after that, stayed away for a decade, and only resurfaced in Eden's Ridge a few months ago. Xander had just proposed a couple weeks back, and it seemed Kennedy was hell bound and determined to be married next month. What was the hurry, unless there was an oops on the way that they wanted to legitimize before the official election for sheriff in November?

Even as the question crossed his mind, one of his waitresses asked it for him. "Seriously, girl, what's the rush? Did the golden boy knock you up?"

Trish Morgan didn't have a subtle bone in her body and was always all up in everybody's business. But the customers seemed to like her—the men for the T and A and the women for whatever gossip she served up alongside their dinners.

More than used to Trish's less-than-subtle attempts at ferreting out the latest dirt, Kennedy rolled her eyes. "No, we just don't want to waste any more time apart."

"I ought to hate your guts on principle for nabbing one of the Ridge's most eligible bachelors, but it's hard to do that when you look so damned happy."

"Thanks. I think." As Trish sauntered off to finish refilling ketchup bottles, Kennedy turned back to her conversation with her wedding planner. As talk shifted to bridesmaids dresses—oh hell, were those fabric swatches on his bar?—Denver flipped the channel of the nearest flatscreen to ESPN and turned up the volume a bit. Hopefully coverage of the College World Series would help offset the estrogen.

Kennedy did look happy. That hadn't been the case when Denver had hired her a few months back, after her mom's unexpected death in a car accident. Carving out a new niche in Eden's Ridge and within her family had gone a long way toward banishing the shadows from her eyes. But fixing things with Xander seemed to have done the rest. Love conquered all, and all that shit. Denver legitimately liked her—had, right from the start, and he liked seeing her happy. He just hoped her happiness and impending nuptials weren't going to lose him a great bartender.

"—in with Misty Pennebaker."

The name had Denver's attention sharpening like a dog on point. Of course Misty would do the flowers. Even Denver knew she was the only florist in town. He'd taken note of Misty and her flowers every day on his drive to work for the last three years. Hard not to take notice of a woman who looked like she did—sort of neo-hippie flower child, with a smile that could light up Main Street.

But he'd never actually talked to her.

When she'd first showed up in Eden's Ridge, he'd been focused on getting Elvira's solidly in the black, after buying the bar from Len Draper, when the old man had up and decided to retire to Florida. No time for a woman then, and anyway, he hadn't been sure a free spirit like her would stick. But she had stuck, proving that there was more to the pretty brunette than her posies or colorful wardrobe.

And yet he'd done nothing about it.

"Even though it's short notice, she's agreed to meet us here to discuss the options," Cayla was saying.

Denver carefully, methodically stacked the empty trays. Misty was coming here?

She'd been in Elvira's before. Everybody in the Ridge had, at some point or other, for lunch or dinner. But, as a rule, she didn't drink. Since he seldom left his sanctum behind the bar, he'd never had the chance to casually chat her up. Not that he was a casual chat up kind of guy. He could've stopped into her shop on Main Street, but what reason did someone like him have to go in to a place called Moonbeams and Sweet Dreams? There was nobody he wanted to send flowers to or buy a gift for. He had no family. And while he'd made friends in the Ridge, none of them were the kind who'd merit the sort of thoughtful, artsy stuff Misty carried in her shop.

Thanks to the small-town grapevine, he knew she was single, but surprisingly little else was known about her. In a place that valued gossip as highly as gold, that was intriguing all by itself. Since Denver habitually kept to himself too, and he understood valuing privacy, he hadn't tried to find out more. So, he'd just been admiring her from afar all this time, as if she were one of the wild, rare flowers she sold.

Denver hauled the empty plastic trays back into the kitchen, then shoved back through the swinging door to check the syrup levels on the drink fountain. And there she was, framed in the front entrance as the door swung slowly closed behind her. She was wearing one of those bright, flower child dresses that skimmed just below the knees of her very fine legs. The slanting rays of the evening sun teased out traces of red in the dark walnut strands of her hair, spotlighting the trademark crown of flowers she wore. It should have looked ridiculous on a grown woman, but Denver found it unaccountably appealing—a fact which he'd take to his grave and beat anybody for suggesting. She just seemed comfortable in herself, quirks and all. He admired the hell out of that.

"Denver?"

He jolted, realizing from the look on Kennedy's face that she'd been talking to him for more than a second.

"I'm gonna take my break to sort some wedding stuff, okay?"

Ignoring Kennedy's knowing smirk, and the fact that Misty wasn't even looking in his direction at all, he jerked his shoulders. "Yeah, fine," he told her, as he turned to the first patron of the after work crowd. "What can I get you?"

* * *

Misty Pennebaker slipped into Elvira's Tavern, pitifully grateful her work day was at an end. Well, there'd be more work with this wedding consult, but that would be fun and for friends. Not that they were friends just yet, but Kennedy bought flowers twice a week for the inn she ran with her sisters, and Misty had hopes they would get there.

She hesitated in the doorway, waiting for her eyes to adjust. She scanned the bar, looking for Cayla and Kennedy, and looked away quickly when she caught Denver Hershal watching her. Even while she avoided it, his gaze had an almost physical weight as it pinned her where she stood. Her skin heated from more than the early June sun, which made no sense at all because he wasn't even smiling. She didn't think she'd ever seen him smile.

The man had presence, and he made her uneasy. Not that she felt threatened by him, despite the tattoos she could see peeking out from beneath his shirtsleeves. He'd never said more than two words to her in the three years she'd been in Eden's Ridge, and she hadn't really done more than nod at him, as was small town custom. Once you were here for a year or so, you knew nearly everyone on some level. But there was something closed about Denver, just one of the things that set him apart from others she had met in the Ridge. He seemed to want to be left alone. Whatever his secrets—and nobody seemed to know what they were, at least not that she'd heard—he had a right to keep them.

Misty saw no reason to push or pry. She understood walling yourself off. Hadn't she done the same? Oh, she'd made friends. She'd made a point of it, as she'd opened her business, gotten to know the various artists and artisans in the area. But there was a very clear line between Now and Life Before The Ridge.

Finally spotting her friends in a booth across the way, Misty broke her temporary paralysis and crossed to join them.

"You are just in time," Cayla crowed. "I've got *ideas!*"

Misty grinned at her enthusiasm. "Kennedy, did you realize you were going to be a guinea pig when you agreed to this?"

Kennedy shrugged. "I needed a wedding planner. Cayla needed someone to practice her event planning skills on to kick off her new business. Seems like win-win to me."

Misty had to agree. A local girl who'd come home to Eden's Ridge after a nasty divorce, Cayla was starting over. Misty knew all about that, and she was all over doing whatever she could to support Cayla's new enterprise.

Over a plate of nachos, they talked budgets and timelines, before finally turning to flower options for the venue—the barn on the family property, behind the inn.

"It's going to be a country wedding, but not redneck," Cayla said. "Tasteful."

"I think Xander was ready to ask me to marry him all over again, when I told him he didn't have to wear a tux."

"You are, without a doubt, the most laid back bride I have ever worked with," Misty said.

Kennedy shrugged, her green eyes dreamy. "I'm just happy to finally be with my Xander."

Propping her chin on one fist, Cayla sighed. "They're disgustingly happy. Join me in my moment of envy."

Misty laughed. "I'm not looking for a man."

"Well, neither am I. I'd like to be more rid of the old one than I am. But damn, I'd love to be that kind of happy."

"Fine," Misty conceded. "Maybe I'd change my mind if I had a guy who looked at me the way Xander looks at Kennedy."

Kennedy squirmed a little. "This is a wedding planning meeting, is it not?"

"Yes, yes, back to work," Cayla said, diving back into her planner and coming out with photos of the barn's interior. "Now, I think we can use some kind of fabric swags or drapes to hide the less attractive sections of the barn, like the hay loft where y'all have stuff stored. And we'll use the crap out of some white twinkle lights and some of that pretty outdoor lighting like you see on restaurant patios sometimes."

"That sounds good," Misty agreed. "And of course, I can use floral arrangements to direct people's attention down the aisle and toward whatever you deem is the front. But it might be nice to have a focal point since there's no real altar. Something to give it some pizzazz."

Kennedy looked intrigued. "Like what?"

"An arbor maybe. Something I can twine with flowers and ribbon. It could be done up really pretty and in your colors."

Cayla clapped her hands once, pressing her lips together in an obvious effort to hold in a squee.

Misty smiled. "I recognize your lightbulb moment. What are you thinking?"

Instead of answering, Cayla waved her hand. "Denver! Come here a sec."

What the hell? Are we ordering more drinks?

Denver left the sanctity of the bar and strode over, his long legs eating up the distance. "Yeah?"

"How much do you love Kennedy?"

He didn't even blink. "Enough not to complain that her break's run over for wedding planning." It wasn't said in a teasing tone, just matter-of-fact.

But Cayla wasn't put off in the least. "How 'bout enough to build something for the wedding?"

Build something? He's a bartender.

Denver frowned, his brows drawing down over cool gray eyes. "Like what?"

"An arbor. Something Misty can train some flowers around and on. I've seen your woodworking. It's totally in your wheelhouse." Cayla gestured to the bar. "He carved all that himself."

Collectively, they all shifted to look at the bar, with its subtly beautiful pattern carved into the side panels. Misty hadn't ever really noticed it before because there was usually a crowd of people blocking it. She wanted to get up, get a closer look, but Denver shifted his gaze to her, pinning her in place.

"You want me to build an arbor?"

Something about the way the question was directed at her—or maybe it was just his intense focus—made Misty feel somehow like his target. She pointed at Cayla. "I want someone to build an arbor. She's the one throwing you under the bus."

Cayla clasped her hands in prayer position and gave him The Face—an adult version of the one her four-year-old regularly employed. "*Please*, Denver. For me? For Kennedy? For love?"

He winced. "If I do it, will you stop with all the gushy shit?"

Cayla crossed her heart with one finger.

Face set in lines of resignation, he sighed and looked at the bride to be. "Fine. What exactly do you want?"

Kennedy held up her hands. "Don't look at me. It's Misty's concept."

Cayla shook her head in mock disappointment. "I swear, you'd get married in blue jeans if not for me. Anyway, you are the least fussy bride on Earth. So here's the date we need it by," she scribbled something on a sheet of paper and shoved it across the table at him, "and what we're thinking we can spend on it. Let me know if that doesn't work. You and Misty get together to sort out the details of what she needs and what you can actually put together in that amount of time."

Misty started to protest because Cayla was totally railroading him, but those gray eyes flicked to her again.

"Fine. Dinner crowd's coming in right now, but I can talk tomorrow. Swing by your shop?"

This big, burly, bull of a man in her pretty little shop? "Uh...okay."

He nodded to himself like something had been decided and walked away, leaving Misty wondering what the hell just happened.

Chapter Two

Some kind of bells chimed as Denver tugged open the door of Moonbeams and Sweet Dreams. He glanced up automatically, noting the assortment of wind chimes suspended from a grid attached to the high, tin ceiling—glass, copper, bamboo, wood, other metals. Something for everyone. He shut the door and listened to the quiet tones of drums and flutes that floated out from speakers hidden around the room. Something dreamy and Celtic that suited the tone of the shop. The space was long and narrow, with wide-plank floors he suspected were original to the building. Displays made something of a maze of wares from the front to the back. It reminded him of the lone trip he'd taken to Ikea—herding you through the entire store before you got to the back and the register. Except this was clever, cozy, and warm, rather than a coldly calculated retail corral of gleaming fixtures, filled with a herd of shoppers. Homey instead of Hell on Earth. It helped that there was nobody else here.

Denver wandered through, taking in the pottery, the textiles, the paintings, the carvings, noting the wide and varied selection. Tiny placards explained, in elegant, looping calligraphy, that all were locally sourced from artists and craftsmen of the region. Mixed in with the photographs, the sculptures, the glass, were fresh flowers and plants of all kinds—a seamless blending of the two halves of her business. He could see how somebody might see that vase and immediately want the cluster of whatever those purplish pink flowers were inside it. A girlie somebody anyway, which was her target demographic. As Denver was neither, he found the shortest route to the counter and called out, "Misty?"

Something thumped. He heard a muttered curse and a clatter and wondered what he'd interrupted. She appeared from the back. It was a different kind of flowers in her hair today—something cheerful and yellow, woven into the two small braids pulled back from her face. He caught himself starting to smile at that before he realized she held her hand aloft, blood dripping down her arm.

He didn't stop to think. He just vaulted the counter and snatched her hand. "What the hell happened?"

Misty tipped her head back to look up at him, stammering, "I cut myself on some thorns, while stripping some roses. It's an occupational hazard."

Her hand felt so tiny in his, but it wasn't soft as he'd expected. She worked with her hands, and it showed in the tiny scars from previous nicks and cuts. He lifted his gaze from her hand to her face, catching those brown eyes that were dreamy more often than not. They weren't dreamy now. They'd gone wide and very, very aware.

Denver realized he still held her hand and was all up in her personal space. "Sorry," he muttered, releasing her and taking a step back.

"I...uh...I'm just gonna go wash this and get some antibiotic ointment."

He had the distinct impression she was retreating as she headed back through the curtained doorway into what he presumed was a storeroom and work space. Feeling more than a little bit bull in a china shop, Denver shoved his hands into his pockets and stayed where he was. That's when he noticed the old dog curled up on a bed in the corner. It was a little thing, a ball of black fur, with pointed ears that trembled as she snored quietly. A Pomeranian mix, maybe. Gray around the muzzle.

"Who's your friend?" he called.

"That's Moxie. She was a rescue."

At the sound of her name, the dog cracked open an eye and peered up at him. Denver hunkered down and offered the back of his hand. Looking imperious, Moxie stretched forward just a bit and sniffed. Her little black nose twitched, then she rose and stretched, worming her way under his hand with a sharp little yap that clearly said, "Pet me, damn it!"

Misty came back out, her hand sporting a couple of fresh band-aids. "I got her when I moved to Eden's Ridge because I was finally somewhere I could have a dog."

Following orders, Denver stroked along her little spine, giving the old girl a good rubdown. "Didn't want a puppy?"

"Oh, I love puppies. But seniors need homes too, and I thought it would be easier to keep an older dog with me all the time. Less rambunctious."

It took a special kind of person to choose an older dog, the ones who were usually neglected and first up on the chopping block at overcrowded shelters. He admired the hell out of that.

"Seems like she makes up for that with sass," he observed.

"Hence Moxie," Misty agreed. "Do you have a dog?"

"Yep. Big old mutt. What my dad used to call a Heinz 57 dog. His name's Oscar."

"As in Meyer or The Grouch?"

Denver straightened. "The latter. Though it was because I found him in a dumpster as a pup, not because he's grumpy."

Misty's face twisted with sympathy. "Poor baby."

"He came out all right. And he's sure as hell not a baby anymore. He's a ninety-pound bed hog."

Misty grinned at that and his brain emptied of everything but *Wow*. She had a helluva smile.

They lapsed into silence, Misty watching him expectantly. For his part, Denver was trying to remember what the hell he was doing here. Oh yeah.

"So, about this arbor," he began.

"You really don't have to do this. I can come up with something on my own. Cayla can be a steamroller, at times."

A steamroller who'd given him the in he hadn't managed to come up with on his own. "I'm in it now. Plus, she'll owe me one. Why don't you tell me what you were thinking?" He listened as she described what she had in mind. Spying a sketchpad on the counter, he nodded toward it. "You mind?"

Misty nudged it toward him.

In swift strokes, he sketched out what he imagined, based on her description, thinking he knew just where to get the wood. "Something like this, maybe."

Misty took the pencil from him and began to add to the sketch, refining some details in the carving.

"Are those their initials?" he asked.

"Yeah. Intertwined in a sort of Celtic knot, symbolizing the whole unity of marriage. Can you do that?"

Angling his head, he studied it, seeing how it would work. "Sure."

She continued, drawing out the flowers she'd add. Denver had to admit the overall effect was beautiful.

"Kennedy will love it," Misty declared.

"Well, all right then." Their business was officially concluded. But he was here, in her shop, actually talking to her, and he didn't really want to stop. "We should probably check out the barn, talk measurements and stuff. I expect that would make a difference to how many flowers you'd need, how big I should make the thing."

"You make a good point. I close at five-thirty most days, and I'm closed all day on Sunday and Monday."

"How about Sunday afternoon? Say, four o'clock?"

"That works for me."

Denver fought back the automatic, *It's a date.* He didn't quite manage to cap the grin as he told her, "I'll pick you up." Then he hightailed it out before he made an idiot of himself.

* * *

Wear pants.

Wear pants?

Misty stared down at the text from Denver. What the hell was that about? But she did as he'd asked, unearthing some well-loved jeans that seldom saw much use in the summer. And since she'd gone that far, she paired them with some hand-tooled leather cowboy boots that had seen many, many years' love. The sleeveless, cream peasant blouse made her feel more appropriately summery. Why was she even worrying about what she wore? It's not like this was a date. They were looking at a *barn* for heaven's sake. It was a...business arrangement, really.

Except he hadn't looked at her like he was thinking about business. She didn't actually know what he'd been thinking, but those gunmetal gray eyes had seemed to look *into* her—beyond the polite and the surface she'd limited herself to. How could a look be both disconcerting and appealing?

And he'd told her to wear pants.

Misty finally understood why as she stepped outside her shop at four o'clock on Sunday and saw him cruising down Main Street on a motorcycle.

Oh my...

Bon Jovi's "Dead or Alive" started up as a soundtrack in her head as he pulled up to the curb and shut off the engine. Despite the summer weather, he wore a dark brown leather jacket that hugged his bulk and accentuated that incredible shoulder to waist ratio. There were racing stripes down the sleeves, which seemed to fit with the lines of the motorcycle between his muscular thighs, currently clad in faded jeans. She couldn't see his face for the helmet, but she knew it was Denver—it wasn't the first time she had noticed the bike, or the biker. Behind the visor, she had the sense he was grinning at her.

Roll your tongue back in, girl.

When he tugged off the helmet, her tongue nearly fell back out of her mouth because, holy hell, Denver Hershal's smile was lethal.

"Hi."

"Hi," she managed.

His gaze skimmed her from head to toe and nodded in approval. "You wore boots, too. Good."

He swung his leg over and dismounted—is that what it was called getting off a steel horse like this?

Misty had never really had an interest in motorcycles, but with this bike, and, more likely, Denver and his leather standing in front of it...that could change. "That doesn't look like any motorcycle I've ever seen. It's way more—" She searched for the right word, and almost said "more" again. "—classy looking."

"That's probably because you're used to seeing nothing but Harleys and crotch rockets." Denver ran one big hand lovingly over the dark green tank. "This here is Roxanne. She's a 1981 BMW R100RT, one of the greatest of the airheads."

Misty had no idea what that meant. "Most women wouldn't appreciate being called an airhead."

That deadly grin flashed again, and she felt her internal temperature rise a few more degrees. "It means the engine is air-cooled as opposed to oil- or liquid-cooled, like more modern vehicles."

Misty made a face like that meant something to her, then gave up. "It's pretty," she offered.

He laughed. Serious, monosyllabic Denver Hershal actually laughed. "Yes, yes she is. My dad and I rebuilt her together back when I was in high school." It was obviously a good memory for him.

"She's perfect for a Sunday afternoon ride and the weather's beautiful. You game?"

She eyed the seat, which didn't seem to leave a lot of room at the back end. "Is there room for two people?"

"Sure. Gotta get you suited up first, though." He stripped off his jacket and held it for her to put on.

Wait, did she really want to do this?

"What about you?" His t-shirt would hardly provide good protection in the event of a crash.

"We're not going far or fast. I'll be fine." He waited until she'd slipped her arms into the jacket—the sleeves came down past her wrists—and zipped her in. It smelled of leather and man. Misty was still absorbing that, when he unstrapped a second helmet from the back of the seat. He eyed the baby roses in her hair. "Sorry about the flowers. They're gonna get squished."

"Guess it's a good thing I own a florist shop." She reached out for the helmet and slipped it on.

Denver crouched down, shifting, tugging, and adjusting straps, until he was satisfied the helmet fit properly. "All right. You ready?"

Her nerves jumped. "Is that a rhetorical question?"

"Ever been on a motorcycle before?"

"No." She shook her head for emphasis and felt like a bobblehead doll from the extra weight.

"You have the easy job. Hang on to me, lean when I lean. That's it. Easy as pie."

"Pie," she repeated. "Right."

"I'll get on first, then you swing on behind me." He put his own helmet back on, kicked up the stand, and swung one long leg over the back.

There *really* didn't look like enough room on that seat for two people. As if sensing her reluctance, Denver scooted forward a bit.

Pie, she thought again, and swung her own leg over, using his shoulder for balance. She was right. There really wasn't a lot of room on the seat. Left with the choice of leaving her butt hanging precariously off the back or snuggling up against Denver's back, she chose the snuggle, scooting forward until the insides of her thighs bracketed his ass. It was a very fine ass.

Oh boy.

"You're gonna want to hold on," he said, his voice muffled by the helmet.

Misty closed the face shield and lightly gripped his waist. He cranked the bike and smoothly pulled away from the curb. This wasn't so bad. Nice and easy, as he'd said. Then he shifted gears with a little jerk that had her clenching her hands tighter. When he leaned into the turn off Main Street, and onto the country road that would take them out to The Misfit Inn, she yelped and banded her arms around his waist, plastering herself to his back.

"Relax!" he shouted, laying a hand over hers, where she was probably squeezing the life out of him.

She forced her muscles to ease a fraction. As the bike gained speed, she tried to focus on something other than the terrifying sensation of not being surrounded by *anything*. What she focused on was him and the curious intimacy of riding behind him. Pressed close, she felt every shift of his body, every flex of his muscle. He didn't have any of her tension. He was a man in complete control.

And Misty liked it.

She also liked the defined ridges of abs she felt beneath her palm. This man was in shockingly good shape for a guy who worked in a bar, and she wasn't ashamed to admit, she wouldn't mind getting to know the rest of him a little better. She wondered if this had been his plan.

The ride was over too soon.

A handful of cars were in the gravel lot behind the inn. Denver bypassed them and pulled right on up to the barn, to a patch of pavement. At his signal, she slid off, using his shoulder for balance again and feeling a little rubber-legged as she stood on her own. He swung his leg off the bike and put down the kickstand before tugging his helmet off.

She did the same. "That was amazing."

There went the grin again. "I thought you might like it. There's nothing like feeling the buffet of the wind and the freedom of the open road."

The feel of the wind. Yeah. Let's go with that instead of the feel of your abs.

Feeling her cheeks heat, Misty looked back toward the house. "Do you think we should go let them know we're here?"

"I talked to Kennedy at work. She already knows we're coming. Said to do whatever we needed to do."

Of course he had.

Misty took off the jacket and laid it over the seat. They hung the helmets on the mirrors and strode inside. He turned all business, pulling a tape measure out from somewhere and getting her to hold the other end as he measured the space, tapping the details into his phone. They discussed placement and height, even lighting. And all the while, Misty watched the easy flex of those shoulders in his t-shirt and remembered the look of him as he'd vaulted over her counter like it was nothing. When was the last time she'd been this *aware* of a man?

The sensation didn't abate as they rode back to town. She enjoyed the return trip more, feeling confident that they weren't going to end up as smears on the pavement. And she saw what he meant about the feel of the wind and the open road, though his body served as an effective windshield for her. She toyed with a question in her mind. By the time they pulled back up in front of her shop, she'd made a decision.

She wanted to know more.

Dismounting with more grace than she'd managed the first time, she pulled off the helmet and shook out her hair like she'd seen in the movies. When the baby roses, now crushed, rained down like some kind of floral dandruff, she figured that had ruined the effect. But it didn't curb her intent.

"Thanks for the ride. It was a lot of fun."

He sat astride his steel horse—Bon Jovi, eat your heart out—and rested his forearms across the handlebars. "Glad you enjoyed it. I'll be getting started on the arbor tomorrow."

Can I come see your workshop? Would he think that was a euphemism? She really did want to see his workspace and how he brought his vision to life. She'd toured more than a dozen different spaces of the artisans whose work she carried. Customers loved hearing little details about how a piece had been created. But this wasn't about her shop. She really just wanted to get to know more about him. So she took a different tack.

"Would you like to come to dinner?"

"I like food," he said equably.

Misty's lips twitched. "Then how about you tell me what night works for you, and I'll introduce you to some of mine."

"Pick any night."

"What about your shift at the Tavern?"

A flash of humor lit his eyes. "I've got an in with the boss. You let me know when and where, and I'll be there."

She did a quick mental review of her calendar. The early part of the week was slammed, but by midweek she'd be done with the flowers for the monthly Pilot Club ladies' luncheon. "Wednesday? Say seven?" That would give her time to get home after closing, do some last-minute cleaning, and get whatever she was cooking going.

"Sounds good."

Misty gave him her address. "You should bring Oscar. I've got a fenced yard. There's room for him to romp with Moxie."

One brow quirked up. "Does Moxie have enough energy to romp?"

"You'd be surprised."

Denver nodded. "All right, then. Oscar and I will see y'all on Wednesday."

Misty lifted her hand in a wave and waited until he'd cranked the engine again before saying, "Can't wait."

Chapter Three

"Pretend you have manners, okay? We're trying to impress these ladies."

Oscar plopped his butt down on Misty's front stoop and, tongue lolling, tipped his head back to look at Denver, as if to say, *See, I got this.* One ear flopped over his eye, making him look a lot more like trouble than a canine gentleman. With a little prayer that the mutt remembered his training, Denver held out the gift bag. Oscar clamped the handle between his teeth and turned back to the door, his baseball bat of a tail wagging so hard, it swept the front stoop.

Man, he hoped this wasn't a mistake. He'd wanted to make a good impression. His grandmama had hailed from Georgia, and, during the formative years she'd helped his father raise him, she'd impressed upon Denver proper company etiquette. It wasn't something he'd been called on much to use in his line of work, certainly wasn't something he or Dad had worried about after her passing. But Denver had heard her voice in his head, telling him he'd best not show up to a woman's house for dinner empty-handed. He'd wrestled over that. What the hell did you bring a florist? Surely not flowers. And that felt too date-like. For all he knew he'd misread things and this was meant to be a playdate for the dogs. So he'd taken a different tack and hoped it was the right one. Gripping the other hostess gift in his hand, and feeling like an idiot, Denver rang the bell.

Misty answered the door a few moments later, barefoot, with Moxie tucked under one arm and her hair flowing loose around her shoulders.

He said the first thing that sprang to mind. "No flowers?"

"Huh?"

"In your hair."

"Oh, no." She raked a hand through it. "I do that as my own form of free advertisement. Since I'm done with work for the day..."

He wondered what today's flowers had been, but didn't ask. Instead, he held out the tiny parcel in his hand. "This is for the lady of the house."

Seeming a little flustered, she took it. "Oh, you didn't have to do that."

Denver nodded to Moxie. "Pretty sure the queen there will disagree and anyway, Oscar brought yours. Oscar, say hello."

Oscar angled his head and lifted a paw to shake.

"Well, aren't you the cutest?" Misty bent and shook, then accepted the bag. "Ooo, wine. Thank you, Oscar. This will go great with dinner."

Bullet dodged.

His dog gave a joyful bark and offered up what couldn't be termed as anything other than a broad, flirtatious, canine smile. She grinned back before lifting her gaze to Denver. "Come on through. We'll let the dogs out back to get to know each other, and I'll see what you've brought us."

Denver stepped inside. Her little house was just as fun and funky as her shop, with a heavy emphasis on comfort. Her living room had the kind of furniture you could sink into, with lots of girlie pillows and soft fabrics.

Misty led them through to the kitchen. "I figured you'd be more of a beer drinker."

"You're into carrying the work of local artisans in your shop. I'm into doing the same with local beers, ciders, and wine in my bar."

She paused, one hand on the back door, confirming his assessment that she hadn't known he was the owner. She chuckled. "An in with the boss indeed."

They stepped outside. Her patio reminded him of some kind of foreign bazaar—lots of patterned fabrics draped to make a canopy for shade and an explosion of lush plants made him feel like anywhere but East Tennessee. A couple of rattan chairs were angled to look out over the yard and the view of the mountains beyond. Wine bottle torches were scattered around the perimeter, already lit and giving off the sharp scent of citronella. Off to one side, a huge gas grill was heating.

"That right there is a manly grill."

Misty threw an arch look over her shoulder. "That right there is a fine piece of cooking equipment that knows no gender. Seems I'm not the only one who made assumptions."

"Touché."

Once Misty hit the grass, she set Moxie down. Denver unclipped Oscar's leash. The big dog immediately turned three circles, sneezing all the while, before dropping into a play bow, trembling with excitement. Moxie turned her back on him, then looked over her shoulder with an expression that nearly matched her mistress. With one sharp bark, she took off like a rocket. In a flurry of paws, Oscar raced after her.

"They'll be fine out here. C'mon."

Denver followed her back into the kitchen and accepted the corkscrew she offered.

"I bow to your superior skills in this department, as I value not having to fish cork out of my wine."

He did his duty, uncorking the sauvignon blanc he'd picked up from Temptation Vineyards, while she got out glasses. His buddy, Ford, had assured him it was a great summer choice, no matter what she was serving. "What are we having?"

"Pork kebabs with summer vegetables and fresh chimichurri. And strawberry rhubarb pie for dessert."

"Sounds like it's a good thing I brought my appetite."

She opened the box with the gift he'd brought for Moxie and gave a delighted laugh as she extracted the stuffed crown squeaker toy. "Oh, this is so perfect for her."

"Oscar would kill something like that inside three minutes, but I thought, being tiny, Moxie might make it last a bit longer."

"She's gonna love it." Misty snagged the glass of wine he'd poured her and sniffed. "And I'm gonna love this. Thank you."

"I wasn't sure if you would. You generally don't drink when you come into the tavern."

She went brows up. "Been watching me, Denver?"

Of course he had. How could he not? But saying so could tread perilously close to sounding creepy, and he still wasn't sure where they stood. "Occupational hazard and a small town. I tend to know who drinks, who doesn't, and what they prefer."

She angled her head in acknowledgment. "Makes sense. I know the same thing about people and flowers. To answer the question you're very politely not asking, I never drink if I'm going to be driving. So, unless I'm home or out with my girl-friends and one of them is driving, I don't indulge."

"Sensible."

They carried the wine outside, and once she'd put the kebabs on the grill, they settled into the chairs with their wine.

Misty curled her feet beneath her skirt. "So where exactly are you from, Denver? Not here. There's not a trace of southern to that accent."

"Lake Tahoe. Though I had a grandmother from Georgia."

"You're a long, long way from home."

He sipped at his wine. "It hasn't been home for a number of years."

"So how'd you end up here?"

Being a bartender, Denver was used to hearing

other people's stories, not sharing his own. He didn't like revealing much of himself. But he could give her a piece without getting into the whole sorry mess. "From the time I was a little kid, my dad and I planned to take a big ass road trip around the country. We mapped the entire route, all the best motorcycle roads."

"Sounds like fun."

"It would've been." Denver's throat went thick, so he drank more wine. "He died before we could take it."

Sympathy flashed across her face. "I'm so sorry."

A waste. The whole fucking thing had been such a waste, with his dad a victim of all the bureaucratic red tape of insurance that cared more about the bottom line than the people it was meant to serve. Just thinking about it had his hands wanting to curl into fists to pound something. But he wasn't going to get into that whole nightmare with Misty.

Twitching his shoulders, he tried to shrug off the haze of grief and old anger. "After he was—after, I set out on my own. Roxanne got a flat just outside town here, and I had to order a new tire. Picked up a few shifts at the tavern, while I was waiting. I liked the look of the place—the bar and the town—so I stayed."

"Simple as that?"

"Is your story more complicated?"

Something flickered over her face as she considered the question. "Not so much. I finally left a shitty job, and I wanted a real change. A friend of mine gave me a gift—this blown glass globe—I have it hanging in the living room, actually—a gorgeous piece. It seemed like there was a different world contained in this thin shell of glass, colors and shapes, maybe like a better world, waiting to be born." A light laugh and a wave of her hand wiped away the dreamy look that had settled on her face. "The piece always fascinated me, so I tracked down the artist—Hale Copeland, maybe you know him— here in Eden's Ridge. I came. I saw. I decided to stay and open my shop. It was about as far from where I was before as I could get."

"And where was said shitty job?"

"Kansas City." That cloud of...something...flickered in her eyes again. "I like to keep my distance from that time and place."

"Fair enough." God knew, Denver understood that sentiment. He sipped his wine and met her gaze. "I'm more interested in the now anyway."

The moment caught and held, drawing out until neither of them could mistake his meaning. Then she smiled into her glass. "Now's looking pretty good to me, too."

* * *

Two weeks, three lunches, a breakfast, two dinners/playdates for Moxie and Oscar, and a handful of random stop-ins on both sides were more than enough to link Misty's name with Denver's in the local gossip pool. Just that morning, Essie Vaughn, sniffer outer of all brewing romances in Eden's Ridge, had been in Moonbeams and Sweet Dreams asking for confirmation that they were dating. Misty hadn't known what to say because Denver hadn't made a single move. She knew she hadn't misinterpreted things that first night at dinner. The man was interested. But he hadn't acted on it, and she couldn't figure out why. This was not a friend thing they had going on here. Well, they were becoming friends, certainly. She now knew he'd played in a rock band in college, that he was a closet *Star Trek* fan, and that he had as big a sweet tooth for chocolate as she did. But that wasn't the only thing between them. So what was the holdup?

At least she'd finally wrangled an invitation to see his workshop. They'd finished dinner—pizza from the tavern—and after a romp in the backyard, Oscar had curled up on his dog bed, with Moxie curled up on his outstretched front legs. They were sound asleep.

"I think we have a bit of a May-December romance going on here," Misty observed.

"A what now?"

"A romance where there's a big age gap between the couple. Oscar and Moxie are smitten."

He kicked back against the counter and looked over at the dogs. "I figure he appreciates the value of a woman who knows her own mind." Something glimmered in those gray eyes as he turned back to her.

Were they still talking about the dog? "Moxie can never be accused of being indecisive." Misty passed him the last plate to load into the dishwasher. "So, the furkids are konked out. Are you finally going to let me into the inner sanctum so I can see your progress on the arbor?"

"It's not put together yet."

"I didn't figure it would be. But I'd love to see what you've done so far. Unless you're one of those stubborn artists who doesn't want anybody to see anything but the final product."

"I'm not an artist. Just a guy who likes making stuff out of wood." Denver shoved away from the counter and headed down the short hall. "I ended up making a few changes. It's a lot of work, so I figured I might as well make something they could use beyond just the wedding." He opened a door into what she presumed was the garage and flipped a light.

Misty followed him into the room. Long work benches lined three of the walls, and the air was scented with sawdust and a faint odor of old varnish. Sawhorses with 4x4 posts took up much of the floor space in front of the closed garage door. Various and sundry other pieces were stacked neatly or in different stages of carving. She could see the knotwork design drawn out in pencil on some. She ran her fingers over the pattern already carved in one arched piece. "Denver, I'm gonna argue with you. You *are* an artist. This is gorgeous." *So are you.* She watched his muscles flex as he easily picked up one of the 4x4s, taller than he was, and showed her the design he'd put in.

"I decided it would work best as a small pergola. They can set it up over a bench and create a little seating area or something. The interior crosspieces will be plain, since they mostly won't be seen. But these, the struts, and the lintel that will face the audience will all have this pattern of knotwork and vines. And there will be plenty of space for you to train actual vines or attach whatever other flowers you decide on."

"Where did you learn how to do this?"

"My dad taught me. He was a cabinetmaker by

trade. Mostly plain and simple stuff, but every now and again, he'd get a client who'd want something really special. Then he got to play."

"You two were really close." That much was obvious in the warmth of his tone.

"Yeah. It was just us for a long time. My mom split when I was little, and he raised me on his own, with his mom's help. My Nana Jean was from Georgia, but she came all the way out to Nevada and lived with us until she died."

"Sounds like a good grandmother. How old were you when she died?"

"Senior in high school. Wasn't the same after she was gone, but Dad and I managed."

It was the implied tone of *until* that had her pressing for more. "How did he die?" she asked softly.

Denver leaned absently against the post. "He had kidney disease." She thought he was going to stop there, but he kept going. "At first it didn't slow him down much. He kept working, kept training me. Dialysis was just another part of the routine. Then he started getting weaker, having dizzy spells, pain. The dialysis wasn't cutting it anymore. He needed a new kidney. I wasn't a match, so he got on the transplant list. But that's a bit like hoping to win the lottery. He ran out of time."

Misty's throat went thick. The story was so familiar, it made her ache in ways he couldn't understand. "I'm so sorry."

Denver twitched his shoulders. "It sucked. After he died, I couldn't stay. So I sold everything we had left, except for Roxanne and his carving tools, and I hit the road for that trip we'd planned."

Feeling the need to steer them away from this conversational precipice, Misty offered up a smile. "I'm glad you ended up here."

"Me, too." She wasn't imagining the warmth in those gray eyes as they settled on her.

"Answer me this, though. If you can do all this —" She gestured at the workshop and the pieces of the arbor. "—why the bar? Why not make a career out of woodworking or carving?"

"Don't get me wrong, I like building things. Using those tools, designing stuff, that all makes me feel closer to my dad. But doing it as a career, I wouldn't get the choice to do what I wanted, when I wanted. I'd get boxed in to those simple, humdrum designs, and that's not the part I love. Keeping it like this means it stays fun and never becomes work."

"I get that. And I respect it. But there's still a part of me—the part that showcases artisans and craftsmen—that feels like it's a damned shame."

Misty traced the pattern again, admiring the design and the hands that had created it as he put the post back in place. She just generally admired the man himself. His gaze came back to her before dropping to where her fingers were still stroking over the smoothness of the wood. Those gray eyes darkened, and she made her decision. She'd made the first move by inviting him to dinner. That had worked out fine. It was time to up the ante again.

She walked toward him, trailing her hands over the neatly stacked pieces, around the edges of the tools he so prized. "You seem to be a very thorough guy."

One brow arched up. "No point in doing a thing if it's not done properly and well. Take your time and get it right the first time."

"I couldn't agree more." She rose to her toes and laid her lips over his.

For an endless second, she wondered if she'd made a mistake. Her heart began to hammer with the first tinges of mortification, as he stood, still as the proverbial statue. Then a growl rumbled from his chest. His hands gripped her hips and dragged her against that big, strong body. He might have needed a nudge off the starting line, but he wasted no time in devouring her mouth. And, yeah, he was every bit as thorough as she'd expected him to be.

She didn't know which of them broke the kiss. They were both breathing hard. Her arms were clamped around his shoulders, and she felt positively boneless. As first kisses went, that had been off the charts. She blew out a shaky breath. "I'd call that a properly executed first attempt."

One corner of his mouth quirked. "I don't know, I might need more data to make that call."

Misty grinned at him. "Oh, well, if it's all for science," she agreed, and lifted her lips back to his.

Chapter Four

"Well, I guess the lunch rush is over." Norm Barber, the short-order cook at Elvira's, perched one bony hip on a stool in the corner of the tavern kitchen.

Denver eyed the half-load of dishes stacked in the commercial dishwasher. "Wasn't much of a rush."

"Ain't nobody wants to get out in this slop." The older man wiped down the stainless steel counters in reach of his seat. "This rain doesn't stop soon, we'll all be keepin' our eyes out for animals marching two-by-two."

Indeed, the summer thunderstorm had apparently decided to camp out over this chunk of the mountains all day. Denver hoped it would blow out before time to prep for the dinner service. Oscar would go stir crazy without having a chance for a walk or a game of fetch.

"Doubt it'll come to that. But why don't you go on and knock off early? Nobody's coming in this last half hour before the kitchen closes."

Norm slid off the stool, already tugging at the tie of his apron. "Won't say no to that. I heard they're setting up for bingo down at the VFW, and I'm feelin' lucky."

Denver smirked. "With the numbers or with Widow Murchison?" It was hardly a secret that Norm had his eye on Estelle Murchison. According to the local gossip—AKA Trish—Estelle had been looking right back. A first since the passing of her husband a year and a half ago.

Norm's teeth flashed white in his dark face as he slipped on his signature pork pie hat. "Could be with both, if I play my cards right."

Denver laughed. "You old dog."

"Don't knock it, youngin'. 'Sides, rumor has it you got a shot at that yourself with that pretty little florist."

Maybe he did, and he'd given it more than a passing thought. But that was nobody's damned business but his and Misty's. He jerked a head toward the exit. "Go on, old man. I'll see you later."

With another unrepentant grin, Norm saluted and slipped out the back door, into the storm.

The dining room was nearly empty when Denver pushed through the swinging doors. Just a quartet of blue hairs lingering over coffee in hopes the weather would clear. Trish could handle them, while he did inventory behind the bar. He'd barely retrieved his clipboard before the exterior door opened, letting in the sound of driving rain and rumbling thunder. A dripping Misty fought with her umbrella in the entryway.

Denver couldn't stop his automatic smile at the sight of her. She'd pulled her hair back in a braid today. The wind had obviously wrought havoc on the original effect, stripping most of the petals off whatever she'd tucked into the length of it. Only a few straggly pink ones lingered. Several tendrils of hair had pulled free to curl around her face, and more than anything in the world, Denver wanted to kiss her right then.

"So there actually *is* something out there that'll turn your habitual frown upside down," Trish observed. He didn't have to look to note the smirk on her face. The tone of her voice dripped with it.

Without even sparing her a glance, Denver lifted the pass-through. "Go refill the condiments or something."

Misty finished wrestling her umbrella closed

and met him halfway. Conscious they were in his place of business and that tongues were already wagging, he resisted the urge to grab her by the hips and haul her against him.

"Well, this is a surprise. I wasn't expecting to see you until tomorrow." Though he'd already been trying to sort whether he could stop by her shop before time to prep for the dinner rush.

Big, brown eyes met his. "Good surprise, I hope."

"Always." And he was surprised to find it was true. He hadn't ever *not* been happy to see her.

Color crept into Misty's cheeks, but she didn't break his gaze and certainly didn't dim her smile. "I come in search of sustenance. I was slammed this morning prepping for a fiftieth anniversary party, and I haven't had a chance to eat. I was hoping I'd scooted in before the kitchen closed for the afternoon."

Of course, this was the day he'd let Norm go early. "We'll rustle up something." He wasn't helpless behind the grill himself. Grabbing Misty's hand, he led her toward the kitchen. "Trish, man the front."

Tongue-in-cheek, Trish just nodded. "You got it, boss."

As he towed her through the swinging door, Misty laughed. "Ooo. Into the inner sanctum."

Almost before the door had shut behind them, Denver spun, giving in to that primitive urge to get his hands and mouth on her. He drank in her gasp of surprise, curling his hands around her hips and yanking her close, even as she rose to her toes and snaked her arms up his chest. He couldn't get enough of the taste of her, the feel of her, of the helpless little whimper she made as he dove deeper. He couldn't get enough of her, period.

And they were in the kitchen of his bar, where they could be walked in on at any moment.

Cursing his own shit timing, he gentled the kiss and set her away from him.

Breathless, she sagged back against a counter. "What was that for?"

"I missed you." It felt strange to admit it. He hadn't let anybody close enough to miss since his dad died.

Misty's kiss-swollen lips curved in a beaming smile that made something in his chest light up. "I have a confession."

With that smile, it couldn't be anything bad. "What's that?"

"I totally packed my lunch. I just...didn't want it. So I came here instead."

The idea of that had him grinning back. "Then let's see what we can do to satisfy your appetite."

In the beat of silence that followed, his gaze fell

back to her mouth, and he thought about satisfying his own appetites with her. When he lifted his eyes back to hers, he found an answering flare of unmistakable lust.

Not the time or place. They were both in the middle of their work days. So he squashed his burgeoning arousal and turned toward the cooler to gather ingredients for...something.

"I don't have quite the breadth of menu options that Norm can make, but I can pull together something. What are you in the mood for?"

"Whatever's easy. A BLT?"

Denver ducked into the cooler to grab the bacon and fresh lettuce. "You're easy to please."

"I mean, anything you fix is going to pale in comparison to the dessert I started with."

Those brown eyes were twinkling at him as he pulled his head out of the cooler. Maintaining a serious expression, he intoned, "Life's too short not to have dessert first."

"I couldn't agree more."

His hand fisted around the rasher of bacon. Why exactly were they still in this kitchen? Oh, right. Because they were both responsible business owners. Damn it.

Striving to pull his mind out of the gutter, he cranked up the grill and started the bacon. "Tell me about your day."

"Well, you'll never believe who was in buying apology flowers this morning." Misty took Norm's abandoned stool and filled him in. The sound of her chattering about customers and flowers and art was a soothing backdrop as he cooked for her. He realized he felt...happy to do something to take care of her. His hands paused halfway through slicing the tomato. He hadn't taken care of anybody since his dad. Hadn't wanted to. After everything they'd been through, he hadn't imagined he'd ever want to take care of anybody ever again. Then again, making a sandwich was hardly in the same league.

Shrugging off the thought, he presented her with the sandwich.

"This looks amazing." Misty bit in and moaned a little.

The sound of it had his dick twitching.

"This bacon is delicious."

Denver subtly adjusted his jeans. "Fresh from Maxwell Organics."

"It shows." She ceased all conversation and demolished the sandwich, then guzzled the ginger ale he'd poured her.

Amused, he crossed his arms. "Want chips or something?"

"No, this will hold me. I mostly just wanted an excuse to see you." She slid off the stool and put her empty plate in the waiting dishwasher.

"You don't need an excuse to see me." He'd like to see a helluva lot more of her—in every sense.

Crossing over, she laid a hand on his chest. "This isn't high school where the worst consequence of blowing off my responsibilities is maybe tanking my history test. We've got businesses to manage. And on that note, I hate to eat and run, but I've got deliveries to make."

"I thought you had a high school kid helping you with that this summer."

"I do, but he's away on family vacation this week, so it's all on me. It's fine. There are only three, and then I'll be blessedly done for the day."

Denver could still hear the drumming rain on the roof. "The weather is really lousy. Can't you put it off until later? Like tomorrow?"

"Nope. Two of them are anniversaries that are today and one is a birthday. They paid for delivery today, so I shall don my life preserver and row my way out as promised."

Denver didn't like it, but he understood her predicament. "You be careful out there. And let me know when you're back, okay? I'll feel better knowing when you and Moxie are settled in."

"I promise." With another smile, she rose to her toes and brushed a quick kiss over his mouth. "Thanks for the sandwich. I'll see you tomorrow."

It didn't feel like soon enough, but he was on deck to bartend tonight. "I'll walk you out."

At the door, Denver watched her with the bright red umbrella as she fought the wind and rain back down the block to her shop. Another massive roll of thunder shook the windows, and he frowned. He really hated the idea of her on the twisty mountain roads in this downpour. That thought made him pause again. Worrying about somebody else wasn't something he'd been doing since his dad died. Looked like Misty was breaking through all kinds of personal walls. Walls he'd erected to protect himself from ever being stripped down to the bone again.

He didn't know quite how he felt about that. She was more than he'd expected in pretty much every way. As he walked back to resume doing inventory, he realized he was still waiting for the "but." Because so much of his life had come with a "but." He didn't know how to trust that things might simply be right, might simply just line up. He'd never been that lucky before.

Maybe there's a first time for everything.

* * *

By the time Misty finished her two, in-town deliveries, she'd given up on her hair, combing out the remains of today's flowers and gathering the curling mess of it into a knot. Her skirt hung wet and limp against her legs, and she couldn't wait to get home and into a hot bath with a cup of steaming tea to chase away the chill. Or maybe wine. It was five o'clock somewhere and she was almost done with work for the day. But first, she had to brave the rising squall and drive ten miles into the county to deliver this last anniversary bouquet to Jolene Lowrey.

Mother Nature was having some kind of a tantrum, lashing wind and rain against the van hard enough to make it rock as Misty took the road out from town and headed over the pass that led to the next valley. She could barely hear the guiding voice of her GPS telling her where to turn, and the wipers couldn't keep up with the deluge pounding down. She slowed to a crawl, leaning forward, as if that would help her see better. The world had narrowed down to a green and gray blur of the countryside. The drive that should have taken no more than fifteen minutes on a good day stretched into a full half hour. Misty's knuckles were white on the wheel as she turned, at last, into the Lowrey's driveway. The trees of their heavily-forested yard provided some shelter from the wind, and for several, long moments, she simply sat, engine idling, in front of the house.

"Get moving, girl. The sooner you finish here, the sooner you can get home to that bath."

Pulling as close to the front steps as she dared, Misty slipped out into the storm. She didn't even bother with an umbrella. She needed both hands to protect the flowers. The wind snatched at her hair as she hustled up the stairs and rang the bell.

Jolene opened the door, eyes going wide.

Misty managed a weak smile. "Special delivery. Happy anniversary."

"Oh my word! You look like a drowned kitten. Come inside." The older woman stepped back, opening the door wider.

"Oh, no, I couldn't. I just needed to drop this off."

"Nonsense. This weather's not fit to be out in, and you're practically soaked. Come in and dry off. Have a cup of tea and cake."

That got Misty's attention. "Cake?"

"It's my test run of the red velvet cake for Xander and Kennedy's wedding." Jolene took the flowers and headed on down the hall, leaving Misty to shut the door.

Deciding she deserved some cake after that drive and hoping the weather would clear by the time she left, Misty followed her hostess into a big kitchen. Lingering scents of butter, sugar, and chocolate had her mouth watering.

"These are positively stunning." Jolene buried her nose in the blooms. "It's been forty years and my Curt never forgets."

Misty fisted a hand over her heart and sighed. She absolutely adored this part of her job, seeing love that lasted. Her own parents had been married for thirty years, but theirs wasn't exactly a model relationship. They tended to operate as if spite was an Olympic sport, and Misty regularly wondered why they were still together.

As Jolene disappeared into the adjacent laundry room, Misty called, "So what's your secret to marital bliss?"

She came back with a towel, one silver brow arched. "Looking to train Denver right from the get go?"

Misty's mouth fell open, her fingers going lax on the fabric. "I...we..." The grapevine was apparently ringing. She knew that about Eden's Ridge, but until him, she'd managed to stay more or less below the radar. "That is getting way, way ahead of things. We're just enjoying each other's company and taking things slow."

"Honey, when a man looks like that, slow is not what any sane woman wants."

Misty's brain helpfully shot her back to that kiss in the tavern kitchen, which had been anything but slow. It had been a delicious surprise that left her needy and rattled and wishing the kitchen door had had a lock. The man was too potent by half, and she wondered how long it would take to work him around to taking her to bed. No, slow was not what she wanted on that account.

Aware Jolene was soaking up her every reaction, Misty made use of the towel and cast around for a new topic of conversation. A miniature, three-tiered cake graced a stand on the butcher block island. Each tier had a different kind of piping. "That's the test cake?"

With a smirk that said she recognized the diversionary tactic, Jolene turned toward the counter. "The real thing will be bigger, of course. But I wanted to test out the layers and play with decorating. I'm afraid my piping skills aren't up to the task. This kind of icing simply doesn't make good flowers."

"It looks lovely. But if you're worried about presentation, you could use real flowers and echo the blooms of Kennedy's bouquet."

She put on a kettle for tea. "Real flowers? I hadn't thought of that."

Relieved the woman had taken the conversational bait, Misty settled in for the discussion. "Yeah, I've done several weddings where they used flowers on the cake. It photographs well and is

sometimes less stressful than piping. We'd just re-
move them after pictures, before we slice it."

"I just might take you up on that."

They discussed options over tea and a slice of
the cake—which was every bit as moist and delicious as a blue-ribbon cake ought to be. A half hour
later, she had Jolene's order for additional flowers
for the cake in hand and the rain had let up a bit.

"I'd better dash before the next wave hits.
Thanks so much for the tea and cake, Jolene."

"Thank you for the flowers and the company."
She walked Misty to the door. "By the way, I never
did tell you."

"Tell me what?"

"The secret to our forty years."

"Oh?"

"We never stop appreciating each other." Her
lips quirked into a devilish grin. "In and out of bed."

Cheeks heating, Misty managed to keep a
straight face. "I'll keep that in mind." With another
wave, she hurried to slide into the driver's seat and
backed down the driveway.

It certainly wasn't bad advice. How many
people got caught up in the everyday and stopped
seeing the little things their partner did to make life
easier? How many let stress and work interfere with
the maintenance of true intimacy? Probably a lot.
As she made her way back toward town, Misty de-

cided she could absolutely get behind a philosophy of always being mindfully appreciative and making time to fall into bed.

Something popped and the van jerked hard. Misty screamed, fighting for control as the vehicle went into a spin. She turned into the skid, certain the screech of tires was the last thing she'd ever hear. Then she was still again, facing a whole other direction. Heart pounding, she lowered her head to the wheel.

"I'm okay. I'm okay." She repeated it over and over, until she managed to pry her hands free and open the driver's side door.

Her legs shook as she stepped out to see what the damage was. The back end of her van hung off the road, and the whole thing tipped at an odd angle. The rear driver's side tire was shredded, and the remaining rear wheel was wedged against a fallen log.

"Okay. I know how to change a tire." But even as she circled around for the spare, she realized there was no way she could get the jack under it with the van in this position. Could she move it to straighten it out? Should she? The road was awfully wet, and the boiling clouds just to the west told her more heavy rain was coming. Was it even safe to try to jack it up? Maybe she should call a tow.

Her phone was in the floorboard. Not damaged,

thank God. Turning on her flashers, she put a call in to Thompson's Garage.

"Oh sure, we can do it. But Willie's got two other calls ahead of you. It's gonna be a while."

Great. She was already shivering from the wet and wishing she kept some kind of blankets in the back. She didn't have enough gas to leave the motor running for the heat.

"Well then, I guess put me on the list. If I manage to make other arrangements, I'll call and let you know."

"Will do."

She'd already been out longer than she'd expected. Knowing Denver would worry if he didn't hear from her, she called him next.

He answered on the first ring. "All settled at home with Moxie?"

I wish. "Not exactly."

"What's wrong?"

At the immediate snap of tension in his tone, Misty winced. "I'm fine, but I have a bit of a situation."

"What kind of situation?"

"I had a blowout and it's going to be a while before Willie can get to me. Unless there's some other tow service in town I don't know about?"

"I'll be right there. Where are you?" She hated the urgency threaded through his voice.

"You don't have to do that. You've got work. I just called so you wouldn't worry."

"I'll be right there," he repeated, enunciating every word. "Where are you?"

Maybe his dictatorial tone should have rankled. But it didn't. That stubborn insistence made her go all warm and gooey inside. She didn't have to deal with all of this by herself. For the first time in forever, she had someone she could count on. A super sexy someone whose worry lines she'd kiss away later.

Misty gave him her location.

"I'm on my way."

Chapter Five

I'm fine, but I have a bit of a situation.

Tension cranked Denver's shoulders tight as he ordered Oscar into the backseat of the truck. He'd come home for a fast game of fetch when the storm died down, but it would have to wait. The dog leapt in, rubber ball clamped between his teeth, as if he sensed now was not the time to dally. It wasn't.

Denver hadn't asked if Misty was injured or what kind of shape the van was in. She'd said she was fine. But his brain readily filled in a multitude of horrors as he drove because he knew better than many that "fine" often wasn't.

I'm fine, but there's something weird on some of my tests. That had been what his dad said. He hadn't been fine. Not even close. Denver knew this wasn't the same thing, but he couldn't seem to stop the churn of anxiety in his gut. The leather on the steering wheel creaked beneath the clench of his fingers. What the hell was wrong with him?

The van sat half on, half off the road, tipped a bit from the flat, but upright and otherwise undamaged. Misty was already sliding out of the driver's seat as he parked along the opposite shoulder. No blood, no bruises, no visible injury, though her cheeks were pale and the hand she lifted in a sheepish wave was a bit shaky. His visual inspection confirmed what his rational mind already knew—she was okay. But he couldn't quite stop himself from pulling her in, running his hands over her.

"You're okay." It wasn't a question anymore. He could see for himself, feel for himself.

Misty reached up to frame his face, forcing him to meet her gaze. "Denver, I'm not hurt. Really. The airbag didn't even go off. The van is fine other than the tire."

Fine. He really hated that word. If she'd blown out two more miles up the road, she might've spun into the rock wall of the pass. Denver rode out a faint shudder. As soon as he got her settled back home and warm, he'd check the other tires and the oil and every other damned thing that could potentially go wrong. When was the last time she'd had it serviced? Who was looking out for her?

But he finally sucked in a proper breath and dropped his brow to hers, feeling himself settle with the contact. He didn't like worrying about her. Didn't like what that said about how important he'd let her become in so short a time. But he liked thinking about all that even less, so he took another breath and stepped back to address the more immediate problem. "We need to get the van moved."

She turned to face it with him. "I wasn't sure if I should move it or if I even could. I mean, obviously it's a road hazard as it is now but the tire is toast. Nobody has been by, thankfully."

Heedless of the rain soaking through his t-shirt and cargo shorts, he circled around the vehicle and immediately saw the problem. The remaining rear tire was wedged against a fallen tree, not in contact with the ground. With the wet roadway, there was no way to get enough traction to pull it straight out.

Denver joined her back at the truck, where she'd cracked the door to reach in and scratch around Oscar's ears. "It's front-wheel drive. I'm gonna hook up a chain to my truck and help you ease it back onto the road and straighten up a bit. Then I'll put on the new tire."

"I really appreciate it." Shutting the door, she stepped into him, eyes searching his face with an expression he couldn't quite read. She squeezed his arm. "Thank you for coming."

Denver laid a hand over hers. "Anytime."

It took longer than he wanted, but eventually they managed to get the van more or less straightened up and out of the flow of the non-existent traffic. He tried to convince Misty to get back inside, out of the rain, but she pointed out that they were both drenched already, so there wasn't much point. Conceding, he hauled out the jack and spare from the back of the van and went to work. Having something physical to do gave him somewhere to put all that nervous energy that had been coiling since she called. The frantic edge was gone by the time he began to tighten the last of the nuts and she'd cancelled the tow from Thompson's.

"You should be all set." Denver replaced the jack and hefted the flat, carrying it over to his truck.

"What are you doing?"

"I'll get this taken care of for you." He set the rim into the bed of his truck. He'd take a closer look later to see if it needed replacing.

"Oh, you don't have to—"

Denver just leveled her with a look. "I can get away in the middle of the day when they're open easier than you can."

Misty's mouth opened and closed a couple of

times, as if she didn't quite know what to do with that. If she thought it violated her female independence or something, that was just too damned bad. He wanted to look out for her, damn it.

"Thank you."

He just nodded. "Go on and get in. I'll follow you home."

She opened her mouth like she was going to say he didn't have to do that either, then apparently thought better of it. "You can at least dry off when we get there."

The rain seemed to have downgraded from thunderstorm to heavy drizzle by the time they got to her little house. He parked behind her van. As soon as the door opened, Oscar scrambled over Denver's lap to race to the van for his own sniff test to verify Misty was okay. Then he spun three quick circles, sneezing the whole time, and bolted for the front door. Denver could hear Moxie barking from inside.

Misty unlocked the door, herding the dogs through the house and out the back. "I'll go grab towels."

Denver didn't stand around. He went straight to the kitchen and started a pot of coffee. She needed to get dry and have a warm beverage. Even as the coffee began to drip, he wondered if she'd rather have tea. He probably should have asked first.

"Oh coffee. Thanks." Misty passed him one of the pile of towels. "Do you have to get back to work soon?"

"It's covered." He'd called in Kennedy to man the bar in exchange for an extra few days off after her upcoming honeymoon. Worth it.

She opened the back door and the dogs streaked in. "Whoa, whoa. Hold up. Paws, Miss Priss."

Moxie barked and delicately lifted one paw at a time for Misty to wipe them off.

Denver lunged for Oscar, managing to get the towel over him before he shook off all over the kitchen. "Manners, remember? Stand still."

Oscar grumbled and fidgeted, twisting to keep an adoring gaze on Moxie, but Denver finally got him as dry as he could. As soon as he let go, the dog rocketed to his lady, barking and sniffing in a play bow. Moxie wriggled, wagging her little tail and prancing off into the living room.

Misty laughed. "Settle, you two. Go take a nap or something."

Her skirt was still dripping on the kitchen floor, her skin pebbled into gooseflesh in the air conditioning. Now that the crisis, such as it was, was past, Denver had a moment to take in the rest of her. The skirt molded to her full hips and perfect ass. The hair plastered in wet tendrils to her cheeks and neck. The cotton tank that clung to her breasts was one of those deals with a built in bra, and it did nothing to hide the nipples pearled from the cold.

A rush of heat shot straight through him as he thought about taking those nipples in his mouth.

Not the time. Curling his fingers into his palms, Denver jerked his eyes back to her face. "You're soaked to the skin. You need to change into dry clothes and warm up." Okay, so his voice had gone rough as sandpaper. He was only human. But he could still be a damned gentleman.

She grabbed one of the other towels and strode over to him, big brown eyes warm and sparkling. In one, quick motion, she looped it over his head and around his neck to tug him closer, until barely an inch separated their wet bodies.

"I definitely agree with getting out of wet clothes, but I have other ideas for how we can warm up."

Now it was his turn to gape like a damned fish. "I wasn't expecting…You don't have to…"

One corner of her mouth kicked up. "This isn't because you rescued me. Although I'm happy to show my appreciation on that front. I've been thinking about this since that kiss in your kitchen. Longer, really."

Well, shit, so had he. He curled his hands

around her hips, loving how the lush curve of them fit in his palms. "I figured to romance you a while longer."

"Oh, you can still do that. But I don't see any reason why that should preclude getting naked together."

Whatever blood was left in his brain drained south.

Misty tightened her hold on the towel and rose to her toes, bringing her mouth within a breath of his. "I know you like for things to be crystal clear, so consider this my enthusiastic consent. Take me to bed, Denver."

*   *   *

At her words, Denver's eyes went dark as storm clouds. He growled, a deep, primal sound that made all Misty's girly parts flutter in anticipation. Then his mouth was on hers in a claiming kiss. No hesitation, just raw need and enough heat she wondered that the water didn't simply evaporate off them both.

God. This was what lay behind that ruthless control of his. Power and a potent hunger. For her.

Misty thrilled at the idea of it, at the taste of him flooding her mouth as she opened for him. His hands curled around her hips in that possessive way she'd come to love, and she pressed closer, feeling the bulge of his erection straining against the zipper of his cargo shorts. She needed to touch him. To see him.

Releasing the towel, she tunneled her hands under his shirt, breaking the kiss long enough for him to wrench it up and off. The fabric hit the floor with a sodden thud. When he reached for her again, she held up a hand, pressing it to his muscled chest.

"Let me look at you."

He was utterly beautiful. Swirls of ink accented the defined muscles of his chest and arms. Before she could do more than run an admiring hand over him, Oscar brushed against her leg and began nosing at the shirt, opening his mouth. Misty grabbed it before he could snatch it up. "Oh no you don't."

Denver shot an exasperated glance at his dog. "We should probably relocate."

"Definitely." She led him into the laundry room.

He eyed the washing machine. "I mean, not what I was expecting, but the height is good."

Misty snorted. "Not where I was going with that. Practicalities before fun. If we throw your clothes in the dryer now, the dogs can't mess with them, and they'll be ready later."

"Planning to get rid of me so soon?" He shucked his pants and boxers as he spoke and her mouth went dry, even as her body flushed.

Jolene was wrong. Any sane woman would want to go very, very slow with a man like him. Preferably all afternoon and into the night.

"No. In fact, I might just hide your clothes altogether." She tossed them into the dryer.

He smirked, the expression surprisingly boyish on his usually serious face. "I'm only good with that plan if you're playing, too."

The quicker she got naked, the quicker they could get to the fun part. "I mean, it's only fair." She slipped her fingers into the waistband of her skirt and shoved it over her hips and down.

The molten heat in his eyes as they traced over her was its own pleasure. When she reached for the hem of her tank, he stopped her.

"Let me." He inched it up himself, trailing his work-roughened fingers up her torso, brushing the sides of her breasts, until he stripped it off, leaving her bare, but for a thong.

Misty shivered, but not from the cold.

Swearing, low and reverent, Denver boosted her up until her legs could wrap around his waist. "Which way?"

"Wait!" Leaning over, she swatted at the controls of the dryer until it turned on. "Let's go."

Breathless from the feel of all his skin against hers, she directed him toward her bedroom. Somehow he navigated furniture and dogs, getting them through the house in record time. He kicked the door shut, right in a pair of over-interested canine faces. Their whines of affront sounded through the wood as he tumbled them both onto the bed.

Denver wasted no time in stretching over her and feasting on the hollow of her throat. Humming with pleasure at the glorious weight of him, Misty tipped her head back to give him better access.

Someone scratched at the door.

"Moxie, go lay down," she groaned.

Moxie barked her protest.

"Sorry. She's not used to being shut out." There'd been nobody to shut her out for since Misty had brought her home.

Oscar barked.

"Hush it!" Denver kissed his way lower, down to the valley between her breasts. "He's got no clue what's going on either. Do we need to actually lock the door?"

"As long as it latched, we should be...mmm... fine."

"Bet I can make you forget they're out there."

"Oh, please do."

He closed his lips around her nipple and sucked.

Misty arched up, spearing her hands into the short, brown strands of his hair to hold him there. "Definitely more of that."

He lavished her breasts with attention from his mouth and those wonderful hands, until she writhed beneath him, needing more. When he finally broke away to move further down her body, hooking his fingers into the waistband of her panties, she almost sobbed in relief.

Then he paused, pressing a stubbled cheek to her belly with an expletive that was far less than reverent.

All but vibrating with need, she met his gaze. "What's wrong?"

"Condom. I don't have one."

Releasing a breath, she relaxed a fraction. "Nightstand. New box. Picked them up on a trip into Johnson City last week."

Denver angled his head. "Really?"

Suddenly self conscious, Misty squirmed. "I mean, I hadn't exactly been expecting to be using them this soon, but I didn't know when I'd get the chance for out-of-town shopping again, and I wasn't keen on fueling additional speculation about us in the gossip mill."

His grin flashed again as he grabbed the box out of the drawer. "God bless a well-prepared woman."

Protection in easy reach, he went back to driving her insane. He was as slow and thorough in bed as he was with everything else. By the time he'd wrung one toe-curling orgasm out of her and driven her up again, Misty was ready to beg.

"Please. Please."

He took his sweet-ass time making his way back up her body, trailing soft, languid kisses on her knee, her thigh, the crest of her hip, before he reached toward the bedside table. Foil ripped. Moments later, he settled over her, into the cradle of her hips. He held there, arms braced on either side of her head, staring down at her for a long moment before he murmured her name and pressed into her, one slow, aching inch at a time. He didn't say a word, just watched her with fierce concentration. Misty could only stare helplessly back, her throat going thick with emotion. There was something else here—a tenderness beneath the heat that made her heart stumble in her chest. She trembled, at the cusp of something so much bigger than simply giving him her body.

Half wondering, half afraid, she reached up to cup his cheek. He turned his head, brushing a kiss to her palm. Then he began to move and she lost the thread of fear in the sounds and sighs of pleasure. Cocooned in the premature gray twilight, as rain continued to drum on the tin roof, he loved her well, drawing out the climb until they both shattered.

Afterward, as their breaths slowed and sweat-slicked skin cooled, Denver held her close. It felt right to be curled up against him, her legs tangled with his. But still, the worry trickled in. When she'd decided to take him to bed, she'd thought it would be easy. An inevitable conclusion to the chemistry sizzling between them. Simple and mutually plea-surable.

But she'd seen his face, felt the way he'd cher-ished her. She could no more hold back her own response to that than to take back the orgasms he'd given her. What was between them wasn't simple or casual anymore. It was more than she'd expected. He was more than she'd expected.

"You're thinking awfully hard," he rumbled.

"My brain is trying to come back online and failing," she lied.

She didn't dare ask him how he felt. Not yet. She knew him well enough now to understand that fast would never be his way. He wouldn't be ready to face whatever she'd seen in those unguarded mo-ments. Pressing him on the issue would be a good way to ensure a swift retreat. And anyway, she wasn't entirely ready to face the truth herself—that she was more than half in love with him already.

He'd catch up eventually. She had faith. Meanwhile, she tucked the knowledge close to her heart and rolled to straddle him, intent on distracting them both.

Chapter Six

"I had a to-go order."

Across the counter, Crystal Blue, proprietress of Crystal's Diner and current pain in Denver's ass, pursed her lips. "I'm not handing over those sandwiches until you confirm or deny the rumors."

"Holding takeout hostage in the name of gossip is a low move, even for you, Crystal."

"What is the big deal, Denver? Everybody knows you and Misty have been spending loads of time together this past month. And don't even try to tell me it's just for the sake of Kennedy and Xander's wedding. I want to hear it straight from the horse's mouth. Are you and Misty Pennebaker together?" She fisted her hands on ample hips and stared him down.

When Denver just stared back, Crystal stamped her foot. "Is she your girlfriend?"

"If I say yes, will you give me my sandwiches, while they're still hot?"

"As long as it's not a lie."

"Then yes." Not that they'd talked about it since he'd stumbled out of her house in the wee hours a couple days ago, but Misty didn't strike him as someone who'd be casually knocking boots without some kind of commitment. They should probably discuss that.

"I *knew it!*" she crowed.

"Then why did you have to harass me about it?" Denver muttered.

"Oh, shut up and take some pie to your sweetheart." Crystal boxed up a slice of cherry and added it to the bag before handing it across the counter.

"How do you know that's where I'm going?"

"Because you ordered the grilled mac and cheese sandwich with curly fries, which is what she always orders."

"So does half the town. It's your best-selling sandwich."

"Yeah, but the rest of the town doesn't make you smile."

Realizing he was grinning like the damned

Cheshire Cat, Denver pokered up. Crystal just smirked at him. Time to go.

"Tell Misty I said hi!"

"You wanted to live here," he reminded himself as he hit the sidewalk. But this was the first time he'd been the center of attention since the year he'd moved to the Ridge. He kept to himself, kept off their radar, and he liked it that way. So did Misty. Well, they were in it now. He'd probably best confirm the status of their relationship himself before it got back to her that he'd up and made a public announcement in the diner.

Denver was still pondering how to broach that subject as he opened the door to Moonbeams and Sweet Dreams. He knew instantly that something was off. Pausing just in the threshold, he scanned the shop. Nothing seemed out of place. Then he realized there was no music. Maybe she was picking a new playlist. He headed for the back.

"Misty?"

"In the back." Her voice lacked its usual cheerful enthusiasm.

Oh God. What if something had happened to Moxie? Braced for the worst, Denver quickened his pace. As soon as he rounded the counter, the little dog leapt up from her bed and rushed over, demanding attention. He loosed a breath and scooped her up, giving her an automatic cuddle as he continued into Misty's workroom.

She sat at a table. Beside her was an open wooden crate, spilling packing material onto the floor. On the table itself was an enormous glass... something or other. It was obviously art of some kind, but that was as much as he could tell.

She swiveled on her stool and mustered up a smile. But it was a weak facsimile of her norm. "Hi." She seemed dimmer somehow, not at all herself.

Denver set the food on a shelf. "I brought lunch."

"That was sweet. Thanks."

"What's wrong?"

"Nothing."

"Are you saying that because you don't want to tell me or because you're trying to convince yourself you're not upset about something?"

The pale smile flashed again. "Maybe a little of both."

He set Moxie down and fished out the dog biscuit from his pocket. She snatched it from his grasp and went trotting back to her bed. Hands free, Denver framed Misty's face, brushing a gentle kiss over her lips before combing her hair back with his fingers. "Talk to me."

She turned to look at the glass thing on the table. "It's beautiful, isn't it? Hale's work. He always sends me something truly exquisite on this day."

"Why today?"

"Trying to cheer me up, I suppose." She sighed. "You remember I told you that I ended up here because a friend had given me one of Hale's pieces, and I tracked him down?"

"Yeah."

"Judy wasn't a typical friend. She was this woman I got to know through my job. I was the managed care specialist at her HMO."

A sick feeling set up in Denver's gut as he grabbed another stool and sat across from her.

"She first called in because of a denied claim. It was a common enough thing. The insurance industry is obnoxiously and needlessly complicated."

He knew that from so much first-hand experience. The memory of all those phone calls and emails began to bubble and froth as Misty spoke, and he had to fight to keep his focus on her.

"People were usually pretty upset by the time they got to me. I can't tell you how many times I got told off. But Judy didn't do any of that. She was the sweetest thing. Said she was sure there was some kind of a mistake and that she had faith that I could fix it. I told her I'd do my best and that she might want a snack because this kind of thing of thing took a while. She said she was making cookies, and we got off on this tangent where she told me all about her recipe for snickerdoodles and how they were her grandchildren's favorite. I took down all of her information to look into the situation and promised to call her back. She sent me snickerdoodles the next day."

Even as the memory made her smile, that sick feeling continued to grow in his belly.

"A lot of my job was sorting out the complicated legalese of contracts—I'd gone to law school, if you can imagine that."

Law school? How had he not known this about her? "I have a really hard time seeing you in a courtroom."

"So did I. That's why I dropped out after my second year. But I understood contracts, and I kind of fell into this job. I certainly didn't love it. Didn't even like it most of the time. But I was drowning under my parents' disapproval and massive student debt for a degree I didn't get. Anyway, so I started digging into Judy's case. It took a while. I had lots of cases. Lots of details and minutiae to sort through. Sometimes I'd call her. Sometimes she'd call me. But we ended up talking a few times a week. I'd update her on the great big nothing I was accomplishing, apologize for the system, and then we'd just talk about life stuff. Those calls were the highlights of my week."

"Did you get her sorted out?"

"For that first claim, yeah. But while I was messing with all that, her condition got worse."

Of course it did. Because that's how it went. That's how these companies worked.

"Her doctor said she needed a particular procedure. So she started all the pre-approval paperwork, but it got hung up. That part wasn't even on me, but I knew the system better than the person assigned to it. She needed that surgery." Misty's voice shook. "I managed to parse out that the problem was a conflict between her primary policy and her Medicare supplement. The procedure her doctor wanted to perform was not the conventional treatment. He'd said the conventional wouldn't work and he wanted to take a more aggressive approach. The way the contracts were written, neither insurer was actually going to cover it without exhausting all the conventional—aka cheaper—options first. Because why on earth should insurance we pay for cover the things we actually need, right? She couldn't afford a three hundred thousand dollar surgery out of pocket."

Denver tasted the bitterness of her tone on his own tongue. Old fury boiled up inside him, making him want to howl.

"I couldn't tell her that. I couldn't tell her that there were no more options. So I put her off, and I researched my ass off, trying to find something, anything that could help her. By that time, we were talking every day. And then one day, she didn't call. And she didn't answer when I called her house."

He knew how this would end before she said it and curled his fists against the futility of it.

"Another day passed, and another. And I finally found it. The damned loophole she needed to get her surgery paid for. When I still couldn't get her by phone, I went to her house. We had her address in the system. I was breaking all sorts of rules, but I had to tell her. It was a young woman who answered the door. A few years older than me. She'd been crying. Somewhere deep down, I knew. But I went ahead and introduced myself and asked if I could speak to Judy." Misty sucked in a breath and blinked back tears. "She'd died two days before."

Denver closed his eyes, fighting back the choking rage. "Too little, too late," he bit out.

"Yeah. I expected her to slam the door in my face. Instead, she invited me inside. She said her mother had talked of me often, and she'd left me something in her will. I couldn't imagine what. We were...well more than strangers by that point, but..." Misty trailed off, struggling against emotion. "She'd left me the globe. It was beautiful. All bleeding colors and this sort of vignette inside that looked like the moon and stars. She said it was called Moonbeams and Sweet Dreams, and it had been one of Judy's favorites. I didn't know then what it was worth, but I thanked her daughter and took it. Then I turned in my letter of resignation. I didn't know what I was going to do next, but there wasn't a chance in hell I could go back to that job. Eventually, I ended up here. I started this shop as a way to honor her memory."

Misty lifted her gaze to his. "Today is the four year anniversary of her death. It always gets me down."

She needed comfort and kindness. Denver recognized that. But he couldn't seem to make himself lift his hand to touch her.

She was one of them. A part of the system that had killed his father and broken his life. An unwilling part, but a part nonetheless. And he couldn't unsee that, couldn't unknow it. He couldn't chain down his anger. Not now.

"I'm sorry." They were, if not the right words, acceptable words. They were all he could manage past the noxious swirl of shit her story had stirred up. He needed to get the hell out of here before he spewed any of it out and made everything worse. She didn't deserve to be the target of his unfettered resentment. "I hope the sandwich helps. I have to go."

"Go?" She blinked, those big, trusting brown

eyes he suddenly couldn't look at anymore. "You're not staying to eat with me?"

"No. I have a...thing." Denver took a step back, then another. "I'm sorry," he repeated, and walked away.

* * *

"It's open!"

In response to Cayla's shouted invitation, Misty opened the front door and stepped into chaos. The cushions from the sofa were scattered on the floor. A bowl of popcorn was upended in front of the TV, where *Frozen* was playing at low volume, and a half-full sippy cup lay abandoned on the coffee table. Even as she watched, a giggling toddler went streaking down the hall—literally. The kid was naked as the day she was born.

A harried-looking Cayla chased after her. "Madeleine Faith, you get your tush back to the bathroom. It's time for your bath!"

Already up to the middle name. Clearly the night wasn't going well. Now Misty understood why Cayla had asked her to stop by her house instead of bringing the ribbon she'd picked up by the shop.

Shutting the door behind her, Misty dumped

her purse and stepped into the hallway. When the little girl came racing toward her, Misty scooped her up and blew raspberries on her belly. "I spy a dirty little girl." Indeed, a fair portion of whatever had been for dinner was smeared all over her face. Mac and cheese had definitely been part of the menu.

"No!" Maddie giggled.

"Don't want a bath?" Misty asked.

"No!" Maddie shouted. "I'm a princess! I don't have to."

"Princesses have to be clean. It's in the handbook."

"What's a handbook?"

Misty began walking down the hall, carrying the squirming bundle of little girl. "It's like the Princess Rulebook. Elsa and Anna are always clean, aren't they?"

Maddie screwed up her face in thought, and Misty prayed she hadn't misremembered the movie.

"Yeah,' Maddie admitted slowly.

"Don't you want to be a princess like Elsa?"

Maddie shrieked a fresh giggle. "I wanna be a reindeer like Sven!"

"But then you'd have to eat hay. You don't wanna do that, do you?"

She made a squished face of disgust. "I don't like hay."

"Then princess it is. And princesses take baths." Misty set her into the tub, which was already filled with bubbles. "And check it. Your mom put in these cool colored bubbles. They're *blue,* just like Elsa's dress!" She scooped up a handful and set them on Maddie's head. "There, now you have a crown."

Maddie preened.

"If you play quietly and finish your bath, you can have two stories tonight before bed," Cayla promised from the doorway.

"'Kay."

"Mommy and Miss Misty are gonna be right out here, okay?"

But Maddie was already lost in her adventure, which Misty was pretty sure was a reenactment of Elsa and Anna's parents' ship sinking.

Cayla stepped into the hall and blew out a breath. "Thanks for that. It's been a...day. And thank you for coming by. I'm sure I interrupted plans with Denver."

It was Misty's turn to blow out a breath. "You'd be wrong. I haven't spoken to him in a week." Not since he'd so abruptly left her shop.

Cayla frowned. "What? Why? Did y'all break up?"

"Breaking up would imply we were formally together in the first place." Which, yeah, okay, she'd thought they were—or at least had been heading hard in that direction.

"What happened?"

"I have no idea. Things were good. Great, even. Or so I thought. Then last week he came by the shop with lunch from the diner. It was the anniversary of Judy's death, so I was pretty down. He wanted to know what was wrong, so I told him about her. And something about that set him off." Misty had played the whole thing over and over in her mind and couldn't figure out the problem. What had she said? What had she done?

"Was he ugly to you?"

"No. He just hightailed it out of there. Left his own lunch in the process. I've tried to call him all week, but he's not answering or returning my calls. I even went by one day, but he didn't answer the door." Yet a new tire had been waiting for her at the back door to the shop. No note. Maybe that was a message in and of itself.

"Have you been by the tavern?"

"No. I'm not going to confront him in his place of business. And even if I were the kind of woman to do that, Trish Morgan is the biggest gossip in town. We both value our privacy."

Cayla crossed her arms and scowled. "That just doesn't make any sense. That's not how it was supposed to work."

"How what was supposed to work?"

"Oh, Denver has had a thing for you for years. So Kennedy and I conspired to throw you two together so he'd finally get to know you instead of just watching from afar."

She'd wondered what that whole steam roller routine was about. "Yeah, well, obviously reality didn't live up to expectation." It was the fear that had kept her tossing and turning every night since he'd walked away.

"Misty Pennebaker, you stop that right now."

Misty had to smile a little at the mom voice. "Yes ma'am."

"I'm serious. You are awesome. And by all indications, Denver agrees with that assessment. So we need to figure out what's got his panties in a wad."

"*We* don't need to figure out anything but the last-minute details for Kennedy's wedding. Seriously, Cayla, I just want to do this job and go back to my shop." *So I can lick my wounds in private.*

"So you don't want to know what happened?"

Misty threw up her hands. "Of course I do. But what if I don't like the answer? What if he decided he doesn't like forward, pushy women? Because I had to make all the first moves in this relationship. I asked him to dinner. I kissed him first." *I seduced him first.* Maybe sleeping with him had been jumping the gun, but she couldn't figure out why.

"I'm not going to make the move to chase after him. That smacks too much of desperation, and I've got some pride left."

Cayla sighed. "Well, I don't like it, but fine. I promise I won't do anything."

"Thank you."

"Even if he does need a crowbar to pry his head out of his ass," she muttered under her breath.

Misty mustered a smile. "Maybe he'll get there on his own. Eventually." But she wasn't holding her breath.

Chapter Seven

Denver opted to do the final assembly of the arbor on-site at the barn of the inn. That way, he could do everything himself and not have to actually talk to anyone. Talking was the last thing he felt like doing. After six years in this town, keeping his head down and out of the local gossip, he'd managed to put himself right, square in the middle. He'd resorted to glaring his employees into silence and otherwise avoided everyone else by sticking to his tiny office in the back, catching up on the books. He thanked God for the fact that he owned a tavern, otherwise he'd have been forced to actually go to the local market and face the masses or starve. In his current mood, starving was the more appealing option.

He backed his truck up to the barn doors and quietly dropped the tailgate. There were multiple cars in the gravel lot, among them Kennedy's. But he knew her sisters had made it into town, so he was hoping she stayed tied up with them long enough for him to get in and out. His plan held for about half an hour.

"Oh my God, it's gorgeous!"

On the ladder, Denver closed his eyes and repressed a curse. Five more minutes and he would've been gone. Instead of looking at Kennedy, he continued to tighten the nut that held on the elaborately carved front lintel. "Glad you like it."

She circled around and looked at the thing from all sides, and all the ooing and ahing was gratifying to his ego. He'd done a damned good job on this thing. She stayed silent as he attached the cross pieces that lined the top. When he was finished, he climbed down and they both stood taking in the finished product.

"I can't thank you enough. I had no idea you were this talented."

Denver shrugged. "You're welcome. The whole thing has been weather sealed, so after the wedding, if you want, you can use it somewhere in the yard—here or at your place."

She clapped her hands and grinned. "That's brilliant!"

He thought about saying something about how Misty had said they could plant some kind of flowering vines to train up it, but that would be opening the very subject he wanted to avoid, so he just nodded and began to gather up his tools.

"Now that's out of the way," she said, "what the hell's the matter with you?"

His hand tightened on the socket wrench and he chilled his voice down to a glacial tone that had cowed lesser men. "Excuse me?"

Kennedy was no man. "What did you do to Misty?"

"I didn't *do* anything." Well, he'd run like a coward and avoided her for a week. That left a bad taste in his mouth, but he just couldn't deal with what she'd told him. How could he look at her now and not think about the reason his father was dead?

"You hurt her."

Damn it. Was this going to be some kind of girl code ass kicking? Denver turned away, putting his tools back into the box. He knew he'd hurt her, and it made him feel like an asshole. But what could he say to her? Hey, now that I know this thing about you that you can't actually change, you remind me of the worst time of my life, and I can't look at you anymore? No. She deserved better than that, and he hadn't figured out what the hell that was.

Kennedy moved to the opposite side of the

truck, right in his line of sight so he couldn't fail to see the pinch of disapproval on her face. "I saw you two together. Things were good. Y'all were happy. So what changed?"

She wasn't gonna let this go unless he gave her some kind of a reason. "I found out something about her past that I'm having trouble dealing with."

"What? Did she kill somebody?" Sarcasm fairly dripped from her voice, but something must have shown on his face because Kennedy sobered. "Wait, did she?"

"No. No she tried to help." She'd tried to help, but it hadn't been enough.

Kennedy frowned, clearly trying to work through his logic without him spelling it out. "Did she do something in trying to help that directly caused someone to die?"

"No. It wasn't directly in her hands. Not really." Misty had done her job. Gone above and beyond, actually, trying to find some way to get Judy what she'd needed. She hadn't set the rules she'd been bound by, and she'd broken them trying to do the right thing. It was more than anyone had done for his father. Would things have been different if they'd had someone like her on their side?

"Then it's in the past. Speaking as someone who's spent a lot of her life being driven by the past, it's best to let it go. Unless whatever it is she did fundamentally alters who she is for you. Does it?"

Someone else would have stayed in the job. Someone else wouldn't have acted in the first place. Someone else would simply have said, "Sorry, this is the policy," and left it at that. Denver had dealt with those someone elses. Endlessly. But Misty had quit. And she'd changed her whole life to build something beautiful to honor a woman whose life had touched hers. The whole thing had made her into the woman he so admired. The woman he couldn't stop thinking about.

Arms braced on the side of the truck, he dropped his head. "I know I need to apologize." And if he wasn't such a chicken shit, he'd have done it already. But finding the words to explain wasn't exactly easy. It would rip him open to tell her the whole thing, and he didn't know how long it would take to scab over again. Or if it would heal at all with a fresh reminder every time he saw Misty.

Kennedy nodded. "I have it on good authority she's working late tonight prepping stuff for the wedding."

"What the hell am I going to say?" Denver muttered.

"The truth," she said simply. "Whatever it is, it's better to get it out there. Trust me on this." When he said nothing, she shot him a piteous look.

"Don't waste the chance Cayla and I bent over backward to create for you."

Denver met her gaze. "We aren't talking about that."

"Are you going to go talk to her?"

"Yeah." His conscience wasn't going to give him a choice. He didn't know if he actually *could* go back to thinking of her as the clever, intriguing woman who made him feel connected again for the first time in years. But he owed it to her to apologize for blowing her off without an explanation. And he owed her the damned explanation, even if it meant baring things he'd kept buried for years.

"Then we won't talk about how it took two nosy women to get you over your own inertia." She slapped the truck. "Go on. Go fix this."

"Yes ma'am," he said and slipped into the driver's seat.

* * *

The wire frames had been a pain in the ass to build, but Misty thought she'd finally managed what she wanted. The pair of them ought to give the structure she needed to hold up the massive sprays she intended to mount to either side of the arbor. She'd be doing most of the rest on-site the night before and the day of the wedding, but having this piece finished was a load off. Her supplier had dropped off the flowers earlier in the day, and the entire massive lot of them were currently residing in the big walk-in cooler, waiting to be stripped and prepped. She'd get started on that tonight before heading home.

Someone knocked on the front door of the shop. She'd been closed for more than an hour. Thinking it might be Cayla with some last-minute wedding emergency, Misty went to answer. But it wasn't the slim blonde darkening her door. It was Denver.

Misty's heart leapt at the sight of him, but she hesitated near the register. She didn't know what to think or how to feel. Why was he here? Knowing he could see her in the dim light, she went ahead and opened the door.

"Can I come in?" His face was back to that stony expression that she knew now was the front he put on for everyone.

Misty stepped back to let him in, then locked the door behind him. "I'm working." Without waiting for a reply, she went on to the back, knowing he'd follow.

"The arbor is finished and set up over at the inn."

"Good. I need to get started tomorrow night."

As he came around the counter, Moxie leapt up from her bed and all but vaulted into his arms. He chuckled softly, scooping her up and scratching her behind the ears while she bathed his face in kisses. Impatient and ridiculously envious of her dog, Misty pulled the first batch of flowers from the cooler. Better to keep her hands busy. She spread them out on one of the tables and began the process of stripping lower leaves, ignoring Denver as he loved on Moxie.

Was this it? Was he just here to talk about the wedding or was he working his way up to something resembling an explanation?

"My father was diagnosed when I was twenty."

Whatever she'd expected him to say, it wasn't that. Her hands stilled on the flowers, but she didn't look at him.

"He was already stage three by the time they found it. Went in for something else, had some scans or whatever, and bam. Everything changed. We were suddenly charting food and meds and bathroom habits. He was still functional, could still do the job, but everything else revolved around keeping his kidneys functioning as long as possible. Then we ran into problems with his insurance. Probably the same kind of shit you dealt with. And while we were waiting for them to sort it out, he slid into stage four."

Misty's heart clenched. Because she knew this story. She'd dealt with this story so many times, with so many people. It was one of the core reasons why her job had been slowly sucking her soul away.

"That's when I started taking over stuff. He had a hard time concentrating. Wasn't sleeping for shit and hurting more often than not. And when the numbness hit his fingers, he couldn't do the work a lot of the time. He started losing out on jobs because he couldn't get them done fast enough. Some of them he just couldn't do, and I wasn't good enough yet. He'd started dialysis, gotten on the transplant list. Things just kept getting worse. And the insurance company didn't give a good damn about it. He wasn't a person to them. Wasn't a face. He was just a name. A file. A string of eventually denied claims." Denver's voice was flat, but she could see the strain in his face as he spoke. She wanted nothing more than to wrap her arms around him, give him whatever comfort she could. But she didn't know if she'd be welcome, so she stayed quiet, listening, as he continued to stroke Moxie.

"I was twenty-five when they basically told us he'd maxed out his coverage. I spent so many hours on the phone arguing, trying to get him taken care of. He had a fucking chronic disease. What did they expect us to do? Nobody had an answer. And there wasn't someone like you on the other end even trying to find one." He lifted his gaze to hers. "I lost my father because the system is broken. And I despise them for it."

Misty thought she understood now. "And telling you my story brought everything back for you."

He gave one short, sharp nod.

Regret sliced through her. He'd been so close to his dad. That had been obvious in nearly every conversation they'd had. She hated that she was a reminder of the worst parts of losing him. Hated, too, that the part of her life she'd tried to leave behind was tarnishing something she'd come to value so much.

Misty spread her hands. "I can't change my past, Denver."

"I wouldn't want you to. You aren't the system. You aren't the one who denied my father's claims. And I was an asshole for acting like you were."

Something in his tone let her know that he had more to say. "But?"

"No buts. I'm sorry for walking out on you when you were struggling. I'm sorry for shutting you out this week. And I'm sorry I didn't have the stones to just explain what was going through my head. You deserve better than that."

The *better than me* was implied.

Misty wanted to wrap her arms around him, offer some kind of comfort. But he still held Moxie and looked very much as if he wanted this conversation to be over. Maybe he needed all their conversations to be over. Even now, he didn't seem to quite be able to look at her. She wished, more than anything, that they could go back to last week, before she'd told him. But it would have come up eventually. And if this was a deal breaker for him, it was better to know now, before they got in any deeper.

"Thank you for telling me." What else could she say? If he still wanted a relationship with her, he had to say so. She wasn't going to force her company on him—wouldn't want to if that company came with a permanent reminder of his loss.

Denver's throat worked and he set Moxie down. "I know you've got a lot of work to do. I'll let you get to it."

She wanted to stop him, to press for more. Instead, she followed him to the door. "I guess I'll see you at the wedding."

"Yeah." He glanced her way, just once, then slipped out the door and clearly out of her life.

Chapter Eight

"I, Kennedy, take thee, Alexander, to be my husband—"

From several rows back, Denver bounced his leg. He was a man on a mission, and he just needed this ceremony over so he could get to it. He didn't know a lot about weddings, but he'd been sure that the florist's job was done once the flowers were dropped off. Apparently not. Despite the fact that he'd arrived early—with several gallons of his spiked lemonade for the reception—he hadn't managed five minutes to talk to Misty. He hadn't even managed to get close enough for five words.

When he'd left her at Moonbeams and Sweet Dreams the other night, he'd felt better having made his apologies. In telling her the truth, he'd finally been able to set aside the noxious emotional brew that had been eating at him for a week. But as he'd come home to Oscar, who'd stopped wagging almost as soon as he realized Moxie and Misty hadn't been with him, a whole different level of shitty had rolled in to fill that void. He missed Misty. He missed hanging out with her and the dogs. He missed talking over his day with her. He missed seeing what flowers she'd tucked into her hair every day. By wallowing in his old wounds, he'd cut her out and left a gaping hole in his life. That was when he realized he hadn't fixed shit. At least not all the way. He wanted her to give him another chance. He'd been all raring to go to follow through, but Misty had been busy with the wedding—the last two days were her prime go time—so he'd had to wait.

Once he'd made up his mind about something, Denver hated waiting.

The woman in the next seat turned a fulminating glare on him. Denver stopped bouncing his knee and rubbed damp palms on his pants. They just had to get through the rest of the ceremony, then he could corner her during pictures. Except once the *I dos* were said and the bride was kissed, Misty disappeared and Denver got drafted to help quickly move all the tables at the perimeter and set up for the reception.

Where the hell did she go?

"Denver Hershal, I had no idea you were so talented!" Essie Vaughn, dispatcher and receptionist at the Sheriff's Office, stepped into his path. "That arbor is just beautiful."

"Thank you, Mrs. Vaughn."

"Where did you learn how to do that?"

"My dad taught me. He was a cabinetmaker and master carpenter." Denver scanned the crowds of people busily placing chairs around the moved tables.

"Such a wonderful skill to have. A dying art."

He worked up a smile because he wasn't a total dick. "Thanks, Mrs. Vaughn. If you'll excuse me, I need to go find Misty."

Essie beamed at him and tapped her nose. "Of course you do. Go right on ahead, honey."

Denver cut a swath through the other guests, making a beeline for outside. Maybe she'd gone up to the inn to help with food? He got waylaid again four more times by people offering praise or asking questions about the damned arbor. Xander's mama tried to talk him into building one out at their place. It took him another fifteen minutes to shake loose of her without being rude. It seemed prudent to make the effort since her son could arrest him. This. This was why he didn't do this for a living. His fuse was getting shorter by the minute. He needed to *find Misty.*

There! Denver spotted her across the barn, adjusting the centerpieces on each table.

Head down, he plowed through the crowd like the offensive lines he used to break in high school football. Misty's eyes widened as he made it to the table. As she'd known he'd be here, he could only imagine he looked pretty intense.

"I need to talk to you."

"Is something wrong?" she asked

Everything. "There are some things I need to say."

Misty frowned. "Here?"

"Yeah." Denver paused, aware of all the people milling about. "Well, not right on this spot. C'mon." He took her hand, relieved when she didn't protest as he pulled her out of the barn.

There were more people milling about, working on transferring food for the buffet, and the wedding party was taking pictures across the yard, but it wasn't wall-to-wall bodies. He kept going until he hit a bench on an overlook a little ways from the house, out of earshot and out of the line of the camera. He paused there, looking out over the mountains he'd made home, waiting for the peace they usually brought to seep into him. It didn't. Peace had eluded him from the day he'd walked away from her. If this didn't work...

It had to work.

He turned to Misty and tightened his grip on the hand he still held. It was daisies twined in her hair today. They were always his favorite. Something simple and cheerful that suited the sweet nature he'd come to crave. He wanted her back in his life as more than somebody to wave to on the street. He wanted everything he'd been too afraid to grab hold of. "I was wrong."

She shook her head, clearly not understanding. "Denver, you already apologized. We're good."

"No we're not. The apology was part of it, but after I finished prying my head out of my ass, I realized exactly how badly I screwed up. Because there's a you-sized hole in my life."

Misty stared at him.

Hell, he was still screwing this up. Impatient, he ran a hand over his hair. "I miss you. And Oscar may never forgive me if he doesn't get to see Moxie again. We want you back, if you can see your way to forgiving me for being a dumbass."

There. He'd said it. He'd put the whole thing out there. Now, heart in his throat, Denver held his breath, knowing it was out of his hands.

* * *

We want you back.

He might have been slow, but he'd finally made a move. And it was exactly what Misty had wanted him to say the other night. But though her heart pounded with hope, with excitement, there was no little bit of fear mixed in. She'd let down her walls with this man. She'd let him into her life further than any man in years, and at the first sign of trouble, he'd run. What guarantee did she have that he wouldn't do it again? That the memories she inadvertently evoked for him wouldn't get thrown back in her face somewhere down the line?

I was wrong.

Did he really mean it? He looked so penitent staring down at her with those clear gray eyes. A rare streak of vulnerability colored his expression, and Misty realized she had the capacity to hurt him, too. This big, intense, broody man was actually holding his breath, waiting for her to answer. Maybe that told her everything she needed to know.

"Having an emotional trauma and choosing to go off and deal with it on your own instead of taking it directly out on me does not make you a dumbass." Misty had worked her way around to that over the past couple of days. She wished he'd told her at the time, but she realized that, in his own way, he'd been trying to protect her from his reaction. "You could have been incredibly ugly to me over the whole thing. I know ugly. I've been used to being blamed for things that aren't my fault, that I had no actual control over. You didn't do that. My story brought up some big emotional stuff for you—stuff you usually keep locked away—and rather than unleash it on me unfairly, you went off to brood on your own. And yeah, that hurt me, so let's not do that ever again. But I can understand it. I even see a strength of character in how you handled yourself."

Denver ducked his head. Was he *blushing?* Sure enough, color was creeping up his neck. "Does that mean you'll give me another chance?"

He'd come this far on his own. She could meet him the rest of the way. Sliding her arms around his neck, Misty rose to her toes and brushed her lips against his. "We can't break the dogs' hearts, now can we?"

Denver's arms closed around her and Misty found herself lifted off the ground as he spun her in a fast circle, before his mouth came down on hers for a kiss that meant serious business. It was the smattering of applause that brought Misty back to herself. Pulling back, she felt her own cheeks heat as she realized half the wedding guests had spilled out onto the lawn and were watching, as were the wedding party.

"Well. I guess they came for the wedding and got an extra show," she muttered.

"Don't mind us," Denver hollered. "I'm just kissing my girl."

The guests grinned. Across the yard, Misty spotted Cayla and Kennedy sharing a high five. Most of those who saw it probably thought they were congratulating themselves on the nigh flawless execution of a quick wedding. But as they both shot matching grins in her direction, she knew what it was really about. She was far too grateful to be annoyed.

Pivoting back into his arms, she arched both brows. "Your girl, huh?"

A flicker of doubt crossed his face. "Minus a week of me being pig-headed, I kinda thought we were headed in that direction."

"We were," she conceded. "But a girl likes to be asked."

Denver's smile spread like sun-warmed honey as he pulled her closer. "Misty Pennebaker, will you be my girlfriend?"

"I'd love to," she said, and lifted her lips to his.

Epilogue

As Denver leaned into the turn, Misty pressed close, her arms tightening around his waist. He loved feeling her snugged up against his back when they took Roxanne out for a ride. She'd taken to the motorcycle like a duck to water. He'd offered to teach her to ride on her own, but she preferred riding with him, and who was he to complain about any up-close-and-personal time of any kind with his girl? And on a day like today, when the sky stretched out in a ribbon of endless blue and the temperatures held the first hint of autumn, it was perfect.

Almost.

It would be up to her whether they made it all the way.

Denver found himself unaccountably nervous. Under the guise of reassuring her, he reached back to stroke a hand along the outside of her thigh. She squeezed him back. Releasing a breath, he forced himself to relax.

Things were great between them—had been great for four months—and he wanted to lock things in. He wanted this woman in his life for the everyday and always, and he didn't need any more time to think about taking the next big step. This was the right move, even if she wasn't gonna see it coming.

Taking the next fork in the road, he wound his way around to the opposite side of the valley, up into the hills just north of town. Sunlight filtered through the trees to dapple the road. It was a picture, one he committed to memory as he slowed the bike and pulled into a narrow lane. Behind him, Misty straightened, obviously wondering where he was taking her. She'd see soon enough.

They broke free of the trees into a wide clearing with a view to part of the valley. The house at the center had seen better days and was out of date by at least a couple of decades. But the gardens that stretched beyond it...those had seen love a lot more recently. Denver drove around to the back and parked with Roxanne pointed toward the stellar view.

Misty slid off in a smooth motion, already yanking off her helmet so her hair came tumbling down. "These gardens are gorgeous! Where are we?" Damn, she was a sight in her own leather jacket and those skinny jeans.

Denver took a moment to appreciate the view she made all on her own before dismounting and tugging off his own helmet. "I thought you might like them. The property belongs to the mom of a customer of mine. She spent her retirement building the gardens out. They were her pride and joy. Her son hired me to redo the cabinets a couple years back, and she used to love talking about them. She's a helluva gardener."

"I'll say." She took a couple of steps toward a row of rose bushes. "What are we doing here?"

"I thought you'd like to see the gardens. They seemed up your alley." That wasn't all, but it was the start to his plan.

"Should we knock and say hello?"

"She's not here anymore. She's been having some health problems the last few months and recently moved to be closer to her daughter in Kentucky."

"Oh, how sad. It's obvious she put a ton of work into them. It's tragic she had to leave them behind. I hope her son is willing to put in the work to keep them up."

So far, so good.

"Go ahead and take a look around."

Denver trailed after her as she moved from one bed to the next, identifying flowers and compulsively plucking weeds as she went.

"You ever want to actually garden? I know you've got your pots and stuff at home, but is that enough for you? Are you basically done with flowers after spending all day with them at work?" He was pretty sure the answer was no. She'd already added pots of this and that around his place. Bright spots of color and cool greenery that added a homey touch he hadn't known he'd been missing.

"I do the pot thing because I live in a rental. And because I had to spend so much time getting the shop up and going those first couple of years. But someday I'd *love* to have a showplace of a garden like this. Oh my God, look at these orchids! " She crouched down and brushed detritus away from some tender pink blooms.

Swallowing hard, Denver stuck his hands in his pockets to keep from rubbing them against his pants. He could be casual about this. "It's for sale."

"What?" Her tone was distracted, her attention still clearly on the flowers.

He tried again. "The property. It's for sale."

She straightened, looking back at the house.

"It'd be a hell of an investment for somebody. The house needs work."

He pivoted to look it over himself, skimming his gaze from the roofline down. "It's got good bones. Needs some updates. Yank down those awnings and swap them for shutters. Swap those spindly columns for some solid cedar beams. Update the paint. The interior's a bit dated, but nothing too much more than cosmetic. There are hardwoods under the carpet, and the bathrooms got updated the same year as the kitchen cabinets. Cindy had a helluva gardening shed over there off the garage, and there's easy room to set up a woodshop. We'd need to fence off part of the yard for the dogs, but that's easily accomplished."

When he looked back at Misty, she wasn't looking at the house anymore. She was staring at him. "What are you saying?"

I want more. I want you. "I think we should move in together."

"Here?"

She'd jumped straight to logistics. That was a good sign, right? Or maybe she was just stuck on pure disbelief.

"I mean, we don't have to, if you don't like it. But your place doesn't have room for my workshop. My place doesn't have easy room for all your stuff. This property would suit all our needs and still have plenty of room for us to customize." Stepping toward her, he grasped her hands, hoping she didn't notice his sweaty palms. "I wanna build something with you, and I think this place has tons of potential."

"You want to move in together?"

Why did she still look so surprised? "I mean... yeah. Didn't I say that?"

"That's a big step. It's only been four months."

Was that the issue? He couldn't blame her skepticism. He'd been the one to let her take the lead almost their entire relationship. But he was more than ready to take this next step. "I don't need to wait when I finally figure out what I want, and I want you, Misty. Morning, noon, and night. If you don't like this property, we'll find another one together. But say you'll build something with me."

Her big brown eyes glimmered with emotion. "You're really sure?"

"Really, really. This is right. *We're* right." And wasn't it a wonder, to have that certainty? "You're the brightness I've been missing in my life, and I don't ever want to go back to the dark. I love you. I probably should've led with that."

Her face melted into a broad smile and she rose up to her toes, pressing her cheek to his. "I love you, too. God, so much."

The sweetness of that swept through him,

wiping out the nerves and the worry that he'd moved too fast, for once in his life. No matter what she said next, he'd have that. He could wait for the rest, if he had to.

Misty linked her arms behind his neck and tipped back her head to look into his eyes, hers full of everything he'd hoped to see. "I'd love to build something with you, Denver. I'd even love to build it here."

Relief and excitement had him snaking his arms around her waist to haul her close, brushing his mouth to hers. "That's good to hear because I already made an offer."

Misty pulled back on a laugh, beaming a smile. "You did what?"

He shrugged. "Steve let me have first bid. If you didn't like it, he'd have just put it on the market like normal, but he was happy to let me have first crack at it. The place is ours, if we want it."

She melted against him. "I want it. I want you. I want us. So yeah, let's do it."

And that was the perfect beginning to the perfect rest of his life.

CHOOSE YOUR NEXT ROMANCE

I hope you enjoyed this opposites attract romance! The Misfit Inn journey continues with *Those Sweet Words,* Pru and Flynn's story, which overlaps with this one during Kennedy's wedding. There's a wedding fling and a fake engagement that you won't want to miss! If this was your first visit to The Misfit Inn, the series begins with *When You Got A Good Thing,* Kennedy and Xander's story.

If you're digging more opposites attract romance, have some one with a side of sexy former Army Ranger and another Reynolds family wedding (that'll be Athena's wedding, in case you want to read her book *Stay A Little Longer* first), check out *What I Like About You!*

Can't decide? Keep turning the pages for a sneak peek of them both!

Those Sweet Words
The Misfit Inn #2

Good old, reliable Pru. Of the four Reynolds sisters, Pru is the natural choice to take on custody of the girl their late mother had planned to adopt. At thirty, suddenly becoming the mom of a teenager means big changes, but Pru's ready to do whatever it takes to adopt Ari. Before she settles down, though, she wants one thing for herself.

Enter Flynn Bohannon, the sinfully sexy Irish musician in town for her sister's wedding. He's led the kind of free, vagabond life Pru can hardly imagine. Definitely not the kind of guy she should be dating, but he's the perfect guy for a crazy fun fling before her life changes. When

Pru proposes a brief, no strings affair, Flynn's not about to say no. But when unexpected complications endanger the adoption, the two find themselves in a phony engagement.

Now they have to convince a sharp-eyed, skeptical social worker, a teen who's too smart for her own good, three dubious sisters, and one protective brother-in-law that Flynn's willing to give up the gypsy life and settle down. But in convincing everyone that this relationship is real, will they convince each other as well?

* * *

Chapter One

"There is no way I'm moving into your newlywed love shack."

Pru Reynolds froze, holding in a wince as the object of the current discussion made herself known. Of *course* Ari had been skulking outside the kitchen. How many times had Pru herself done the same as a child? There never seemed to be another option when the grown-ups were deciding your fate without consulting you. She'd hated it. Hated being at the mercy of a bunch of relative strangers—even well-intentioned ones. But that's what it was to be part of the foster system. That was the fate that Pru and her sister, Kennedy, were trying to save Ari from.

Pru turned to face the girl, taking in the dark, stormy eyes and the mulish set to her mouth. "Nothing's been decided, sugar. We aren't going to make that decision for you." It was important to get that out there. To make Ari understand that she had a choice here. Foster kids had so few actual choices, and fighting that sense of powerlessness was one of the biggest hurdles to overcome.

"Yeah," Kennedy added. "We were just reviewing your options, discussing the pros and cons, so we could present them in a nice, organized fashion."

Ari arched one eyebrow in a move that displayed all of her barely teenaged disdain. Not yet fourteen, she was going to be a pistol, as their mother used to say.

Pru rode out the instant lash of pain at the thought of Joan. It had been just under four months since they'd lost her to a car accident. Just under four months since she and her three sisters had taken charge of the girl Joan had been in the process of adopting. Joan had meant Ari to be one of them—the last and youngest Reynolds sister. But the legalities hadn't been finished, so Pru and Kennedy, and Kennedy's fiancé, Xander, had all undergone the necessary certification classes to serve as her foster parents. Not something Pru had expected to be doing at thirty—prospectively taking on a teenaged daughter. But she'd be damned if she'd let the girl go back into the system. Ari was family.

"Come on and sit down. We'll talk about this," Pru told her.

Ari crossed her arms, but she came over and plopped down at the big farmhouse table.

"Do you want tea?" Pru asked.

One shoulder lifted in a shrug. "Sure."

Pru moved to the stove and reminded herself that the attitude was better than the complete, withdrawn silence after Joan's death.

"So, here's the deal, kiddo," Kennedy began. "The great state of Tennessee has officially declared Pru, me, and Xander fit as foster parents. Well, we've passed all the classes, anyway."

Pru pulled mugs from the cabinet and began to fill tea balls with the loose leaf black tea she favored. "The next step is the home study, so we have to let Mae know whether she'll be doing that on me or on Kennedy and Xander. All of us are more than willing, so it's your choice."

Their situation was highly unusual. Officially, they shouldn't have had Ari at all until all the certifications had been passed and the home study completed. But their mother had been a foster parent for more than twenty-five years and a social worker before that. Mae Bradley, Ari's case worker, had known Joan all that time, and on Joan's death, she'd pulled some strings with the powers that be, convincing them that it was in the best interest of the child to stay put with someone familiar. God bless small towns.

"You're getting married this weekend and going off on your honeymoon to Timbuktu—" Ari said.

"The UK," Kennedy corrected, smiling a little as Pru set a mug of tea in front of her.

"—and I'm not gonna be moving in when you get back and stepping all over your newlywed toes. I *like* you and Xander. Why would I do that to you? Congratulations, Mr. and Mrs. Kincaid. Welcome home! And oh, by the way, here's your teenager! That'd put an end to the honeymoon right quick."

Kennedy reached out to cover the girl's hand with her own. "Ari, Xander and I love you. It wouldn't be like that."

Ari pulled away, wrapping her hands around the mug Pru gave her. "You and Xander lost ten years. You deserve some time to be just together."

Pru couldn't argue with the truth of that. But it was Kennedy who'd first managed to pull Ari out of her shell after the funeral, so maybe she was the best sister for the job. Pru didn't care to analyze the pang she felt at that thought. "The home study will take some time. I expect, if you wanted it, Mae would be happy to do home studies on all of us. Then, you could stay with me, while the lovebirds have their time, and go to them when you felt like you were ready."

Ari was already shaking her head. "I want to stay here, with you. I want to keep my room and help with the inn." She dropped her gaze to her mug, jiggling the tea ball. When she spoke again, her voice was small. "You were there from the beginning, and I want to be a Reynolds, not a Kincaid."

Pru's throat went thick. She exchanged a glance with Kennedy, who nodded slightly. "Then that's what we'll do."

Ari looked up and the guarded hope on her face cut Pru to the bone. "Really? You'll really adopt me, like Joan was going to?"

It wasn't a decision she made lightly. She knew what it meant to be wanted, to have the stability of a good forever home. Joan had done that for her, for her sisters, and provided a safe place to land for countless others, over the years. Pru might not have any intention of stepping fully into her mother's shoes, but for this one child, she'd do whatever it took.

"If that's what you want, then yeah. I'd like that. I'd like that very much."

Ari grinned, her temper fading with the speed of a summer storm. "Then I guess I'll have to start working on calling you Mom."

The word hit Pru in the chest like a sucker punch. Mom. She was going to be a mom. This was going to be her daughter. She was going to be fully responsible for another person's...everything. Holy crap.

"It'll take us both some getting used to," she managed.

Ari slid off the bench and came around the table to give Pru a quick hug. She wasn't touch shy like so many kids Pru had known, so Pru gave her a hearty squeeze, as her own mother would have done. Over the girl's thin shoulder, she saw Kennedy beaming.

"Just to try out my mom voice, have you done your sweep of the guest rooms to see if any of the TP or linens or complimentary toiletries need re-stocking before the next guests arrive?"

"Not yet."

"Hop to. The Johnsons are supposed to be here by six-thirty."

Ari saluted and scurried off.

"Congratulations, Mom. And you even did it without the baby weight," Kennedy teased.

Pru sagged back in her chair. "Jesus."

Her sister sobered. "Are you really okay with this?"

"Yes. I wouldn't have told her I'd do it, if I wasn't. I'm just...a little overwhelmed." And a little bit jealous that she'd be doing this alone.

Oh, Kennedy and Xander would help out. So would her other sisters, Athena and Maggie, whenever they were in town. But there'd be no husband helping her share the load or the joys. She envied Kennedy that. She'd assumed she'd meet someone eventually, but Eden's Ridge was a tiny town, with a shallow dating pool. Unlike her sisters, she hadn't left, other than to finish her training as a massage therapist. Eden's Ridge was home. She'd found no grand passion here, and up until they'd begun planning Kennedy's whirlwind wedding, Pru had been fine with that.

She'd be fine with it again. Her mother had led a full and rich life without partner. She could do the same. If she felt a twinge of self-pity at that, she shoved it away. Ari was the priority. Taking care of her was what Joan would have wanted.

"It's a big step," Kennedy said. "I'd be worried if you didn't feel a little overwhelmed."

"That's probably been a little exacerbated by the fact that we've planned your wedding in a month. Thank God for Cayla Black." A friend from high school, Cayla was divorced and back in the

Ridge with her four-year-old daughter, trying to get an event planning business off the ground. She'd jumped at the chance to use Kennedy as a guinea pig.

"She is, indeed, awesome," Kennedy concurred. "I don't even think Maggie could've done better."

"It helps that you don't care too much about the details beyond being married to Xander in the end."

"True enough. Speaking of, I want to swing by the house to see my other half before I head into work for the night." She rose and came around to hug Pru herself. "Mom would love that you're doing this for Ari."

"I know. And it helps a little bit. She feels kind of like a last piece of Mom."

"Are you gonna call Maggie and Athena to tell them the news?"

"They'll be here in two days for wedding festivities. I'll tell them in person. Go forth and squeeze in whatever canoodling you can manage."

Kennedy rolled her eyes. "Canoodling. You sound like Ari."

"Fitting since she's going to be mine." Pru felt another flutter in her belly. That would stop being scary at some point, right?

"Touché. Love you, Pru."

"Love you back."

When she was gone, Pru took their tea—now

cold—and dumped it out. She popped her own into the microwave, then carried the mug back to her room. Formerly her mother's room. She'd moved in formally after she and her sisters had converted the old Victorian into a bed and breakfast to save the family estate. It was a long way from profitable yet, but they'd had steady bookings since they opened Memorial Day weekend and plenty more that stretched out well into the fall.

Sinking down into the overstuffed chair, she tugged open the drawer and pulled out the photo album with "My Kids" embossed across the front. She'd found it in the course of cleaning out. This book contained photos of every single child her mother had fostered over the years. There were so many.

Had her mother felt this bone deep panic at the beginning? Wondering whether she could do this? Whether she'd irrevocably mess these kids up? Or had she always been the unflappable, down-to-earth woman Pru remembered? With the weight of the decision she'd just made pressing down, she needed her mother's comfort. So, tea in hand, she opened the cover and slid into memory.

* * *

"What's the status update on the wedding?"

"For God's sake, Maggie, we've been here all of five minutes. Can't you wait to try to run things until we've had some time to breathe?" Athena complained.

Maggie shot her a cool look. "The wedding is in five days. There's no time to relax."

And my sisters are officially home, Pru thought.

"We hired a wedding planner. And Pru's here. Shit's being handled. Right?" Athena looked to Pru for confirmation.

Her lips twitched. "Shit is, indeed, being handled." That her sisters trusted her to do exactly that was both flattering and maddening.

"See there? Now relax, woman." Athena flopped down on the overstuffed sofa.

"Might I remind you that there are little ears present, so perhaps tone things down from the language you use in your restaurant kitchen?" Pru suggested.

Ari and Athena both rolled their eyes.

"Gordon Ramsey is worse," Ari said. When Pru arched a brow, she just shrugged. "What? I really like *Kitchen Nightmares.*"

There was no need to ask who got her hooked on that.

"Oh, did you see that episode with that poser in Ohio?" Athena asked.

"'I can cook, Joe,'" Ari said, in a passable parody of the celebrity chef.

"That was *brutal*," Athena agreed.

"Well deserved," Ari pronounced.

Deciding she was just grateful the two were bonding, Pru turned her attention to Maggie. "To answer your question, everything is going fine. Our bridesmaid dresses are ready and waiting. You and Athena have your final fitting tomorrow. The photographer is lined up, and Mrs. Lowrey, from church, is making the cake."

"You're not doing the cake?" Ari asked Athena.

"I'm a chef, not a baker. I *can* bake. I choose not to."

"Plus, Mrs. Lowrey makes the *best* red velvet cake in the state," Kennedy announced, sailing into the room with a tray of drinks from the kitchen. "She has a blue ribbon from the state fair that says so."

"What about music?" Maggie asked.

"My friend, Flynn, will be playing."

"Oh, did you finally talk to him about it?" Pru had heard plenty about the Irish musician Kennedy had toured with for a while, during her time abroad. He'd been one of the first to book a room after they opened the inn.

"No. He's playing his way down the East coast. Not quite sure where he is just now, and his cell phone doesn't work in the States. But he'll be here in a couple of days. It's not like he's going to say no. It's my *wedding*."

Maggie pinched the bridge of her nose and moved her mouth in something that might have been a silent prayer or a curse. "Okay, so what's left?"

"Just decorating the barn for the ceremony and getting tables set up for the reception. And we'll have help with that. Everybody who's got a room booked from tomorrow through the weekend is one of Mom's former fosters. And there are more coming in day of," Pru told her.

Maggie's shoulders relaxed a little. Kennedy swung an arm around them. "Did you think you were going to have to wade in and sort out chaos?"

"It wouldn't be the first time. But I should have known better. I can always rely on Pru to have my back." She flashed a grateful smile.

Pru just shrugged. "It's what I do."

"Is there anything else I need to know about?"

From the sofa, Ari began to bounce.

"You got ants in your pants, kid?" Athena asked.

Ari looked at Pru, and it was impossible to hold back the smile.

"She's excited because she's finally going to be a Reynolds. I'm adopting her."

"Whoa." Athena hooked Ari around the neck and pulled her into a headlock. "Welcome to the family, kid."

Maggie smiled at the giggling teen, who was digging her fingers into Athena's sides in a vain effort to tickle her. "That's wonderful."

"There are still some steps to go through, but that's the plan," Pru said.

The doorbell rang.

"Are we expecting more guests?" Kennedy asked. "I didn't think we had anybody else booked for tonight."

"Not guests. Your surprise," Pru said. "Ari, you want to go get the door?"

"'Kay!" Red-faced and gasping, she rolled off the sofa and raced out of the room. Moments later, she came back, a smiling blonde in tow.

"Hail, hail, the gang's all here," the blonde called. "Welcome home, y'all."

"Abbey Whittaker! I had no idea you were back in the Ridge." Maggie crossed the room to give her a hug.

"Only been back a couple of weeks. Grandaddy Whittaker isn't doing so great. His dementia is getting worse, so I came back to help out, while the family figures out what to do about it."

"I'm so sorry to hear that. But I'm definitely glad to see you. Weren't you off in Atlanta?"

"That's where I headed when Pru and I fin-ished school, but I wound up moving to Mississippi last year. I've got kin in Wishful—Granddaddy's brother and his branch of the family are there. I've been working at a swank spa in Wishful."

"Which is why she's here tonight," Pru said. "She's giving all of us spa treatments."

"All natural and guaranteed to rejuvenate and relax."

Athena jerked a thumb at Maggie. "This one definitely needs to relax."

Abbey laughed. "And what about the bride to be?"

"Pretty sure she's the most laid back one here," Pru said.

"She's in luuuuuurve," Ari sang.

"It shows. Hard to duplicate that kind of glow with even the best products. You look great."

Kennedy beamed. "Thanks. Being happy agrees with me."

"The regular nookie doesn't hurt," Athena added.

Pru clapped her hands over Ari's ears. "Athena!"

"What? It's true."

Ari tugged the hands away. "Joan already had the talk with me. Great sex between mature, com-mitted individuals is good for your mental health."

Pru's mouth fell open, but nothing came out. Her face felt frozen somewhere between horror and laughter.

"Well, she's not wrong," Kennedy admitted.

Maybe that's what's wrong with me. No great sex in.... Have I ever had truly great sex? When was the last time I had even mediocre sex? Oh, dear God, why am I thinking about this now?

Cheeks burning, Pru looked at Abbey, who was valiantly trying not to snicker. "Our mom was really big on female empowerment. But for you, young lady, that can wait until you're twenty-five." She grabbed Ari by the shoulders and marched her toward the kitchen, laughter in their wake as everyone trailed behind.

Abbey unloaded the bags she'd brought and began mixing ingredients, while Kennedy rounded up a bunch of towels. As she created multiple bowls of fragrant glop, Abbey scanned them all. "So, other than the bride, who else is tripping down the relationship highway? Or dating? Or anything involving the prospect of a significant other? Because I most definitely am not, and I need to live vicariously through somebody."

"Those Mississippi boys not doing it for you?" Athena asked.

"There's one very serious problem with them— it seems all the good ones are taken."

"It's a definite problem in small towns," Pru agreed. "I can't remember the last time I had a date."

"Didn't you go out with Gavin Harkness around Christmas?" Maggie asked.

"I went to dinner with him. For what I *thought* was just a meal between joint committee members for that Angel Tree fundraiser. I didn't realize he thought it was a date until he tried to kiss me when he brought me home. I turned my face at the last second and he hit my cheek. Then he just kind of froze there for several seconds, until I managed to twist the doorknob and escape. It was...awkward."

"Well, it's not like the city is any better for prospects," Maggie said. "In L.A., everybody meets people with an eye for how they can be used to further their career. There's no such thing as a simple girl meets guy on an elevator and gets asked to dinner, for a night of conversation about mutual interests. Instead, he's asking enough questions during the salad course, you feel like you're in the middle of a job interview."

Abbey grimaced. "That sounds awful. Please tell me you skipped dessert."

"I gave serious thought to disappearing to the bathroom and never coming back. But he knew my boss, as it turns out, so I stuck it out."

"What about you, Athena?" Abbey asked.

"I intimidate men."

"Shocker," Kennedy murmured.

The impact of the middle finger Athena shot up was somewhat mitigated by the bright green avocado mask smeared all over her face.

"So, other than the bride, we're all failing in the dating department. Y'all, this is a sad state of affairs. We are smart, sexy, available women. What is wrong with all these men?" Abbey came back to the table, passing out warm, wet wash cloths. "Everybody wipe off your mask with firm, downward strokes from the center line of your face."

Kennedy rubbed at the bentonite clay mask already flaking off her face. "Maybe I should hook y'all up with some of Xander's single friends. All of his groomsmen are available."

"Please," Athena snorted. "Porter was one of our brothers."

"That still leaves Logan and Jonah," Kennedy pointed out.

"Athena and I don't live here, so that seems a pointless effort. But maybe one of them would suit Pru." Maggie angled her head, studying Pru from across the table.

"Hello, I'm sitting right here and *not* looking for a setup, thanks very much. I do not need a pity date. I haven't even thought about dating—" She cut herself off before *since Mom died* could spill out. No reason to drag the group down. "Besides, I've got enough on my plate with the inn and the fact that I'm acquiring a teenager."

"Yeah, but at least I came housebroken," Ari said.

"Girl's got a point. Men are so much harder to train than dogs," Athena agreed. She patted her face dry. "Dude, my skin feels amazing."

"Mine's all tingly," Maggie said.

Abbey set a small bowl on the table. "Here, each of you slather some of this on. It's specially made moisturizer. No chemicals."

"It feels wonderful. All of it does," Pru said. "You know, a lot of my massage clients would love this. What would you think about doing some freelance spa treatments, while you're here? We could set up some space for you to work out of."

"That would be wonderful. The Babylon is holding my job, but it would be great to keep my hand in things. Plus, I'll need a break from Granddaddy."

"Great. We'll set a time after the wedding to discuss terms."

"Sounds like a plan." Abbey removed the double boiler she'd had simmering at the stove. "Now, who wants a paraffin bath for your hands?"

* * *

Flynn Bohannon lived a gypsy's life, traveling from town to town, venue to venue, sharing the music of his homeland. To his way of thinking, there was nothing better than seeing new faces, new places, every few days. If things began to feel a little stale, he picked up stakes and found somewhere new. Sometimes he traveled in a group, jamming with other musicians he met along the way. Other times, like now, he was a solo act. Either worked fine for him. It was all about the music.

He'd landed in Boston three weeks before and had been working his way down the Eastern seaboard, playing in pubs, bars, taverns, and coffee shops—a different town or city every night. Some shows had been pre-booked. Others, like the pick-up session he'd had in that pub in Baltimore, where the bartender had turned out to be the cousin of a friend of his mother's, had been a delightful, impulsive surprise. Flynn liked surprises. Which was why he'd made his way to Eden's Ridge, Tennessee a day early.

He'd wanted to surprise one of his dearest friends. And, he admitted, he hoped to catch her before she'd put on her *everything's fine* face and get a real read on how she was doing. Kennedy Reynolds had been every bit the gypsy he was, and now she'd come home and decided to settle here out of family obligation. Not that he frowned on that.

There was a child involved. But he wondered how long it would take her to feel choked by the roots she'd long ago escaped.

It was beautiful. He'd give her that. These were younger, wilder mountains than he was used to. There simply weren't this many trees in the mountains of Ireland. At home, the peaks had been whittled down by wind and weather and time, until they'd been reduced to their bare essentials. Wild, yes, but often barren but for the grasses and scrub. Here the trees stretched in a lush, green blanket as far as the eye could see. As he navigated the switchbacks, he noted the craggy rocks peeking through here and there, but otherwise, everything was alive with the vibrant colors of summer.

The house was set back in the trees, a charming Victorian painted a mystical greenish gray, with crisp, white trim. He'd have recognized it from Kennedy's description, even without the wooden sign above the porch proclaiming The Misfit Inn. It rose a towering three stories high, with a turret to one side. The porch wrapped all the way round, with fanciful scrollwork at the corners and various groupings of chairs or gliders set to take in the view, which was magnificent from nearly all angles. There was the old bodock tree Kennedy had used to sneak in and out of the house as a girl. And beyond it, the barn, doors thrown wide.

Flynn found a place to park and climbed out. He knocked on the big front door, and when no one answered, he circled around back, scanning for Kennedy's familiar blonde head. He followed sounds of music—a cheerful country tune about some lass calling dibs—into the barn. The space inside was clear. White drapes had been hung above to block off what he presumed was a hay loft. Dozens of folding chairs were stacked to one side. And in the center of the barn, at the top of a ladder, a woman stretched to wrap white twinkle lights around a barn rafter. As he stood, undetected, she joined in the chorus with cheerful alto.

Charmed, he stayed where he was, watching. She was all soft curves, a fact made evident by the stretch of shorts across her perfect, lush backside. Flynn took a moment of reverence for that magnificent ass, captivated by the gentle flex of it as she worked and twitched her hips to the rhythm on the radio. *Now* that *is a woman.* He'd know, as he'd made quite the study of them the world over.

The ass ended in tanned legs and sport sandals. Stifling an appreciative murmur, Flynn lifted his gaze higher, noting the swatch of olive skin between the waistband of her shorts and the t-shirt riding high as she reached to continue the wrap. He realized then that she was far too short to be doing this. She'd gone above that last safety step of the ladder trying to reach the beam well above her head. Even as he thought to speak up, the ladder began to wobble. The woman sucked in a breath, flailing for any kind of purchase.

Flynn leapt forward as the ladder toppled and the woman screamed. He didn't exactly catch her so much as break her fall, but he managed to wrap his arms around her as she crashed down, softening the impact as they both hit the ground. They both lay there, stunned, wrapped in a tangle. As she lifted her head and trained those wide, dark eyes on his, Flynn couldn't help but think his breathlessness and pounding heart weren't entirely from the collision.

I'm callin' dibs, indeed.

He couldn't stop himself from reaching out to brush the hair back from that exquisite face. "Are you all right, then?"

"Flynn?"

Well, and wasn't it a fine thing to hear his name on those lips, in that soft Southern twang? As if she'd been waiting just for him, for this moment. The sound of it did something to him, plucking some chord deep in his soul until it sang. Could she feel it where her hands pressed against his chest?

"You're early," she said.

"Seems to me, I'm right on time."

Her pupils sprang wide at that, and she sucked

in a breath. His gaze dropped to those lips, and his hand tightened at the curve of her waist. Only the sound of running footsteps kept him from leaning in to taste her.

"I heard a crash. What—Oh my God, Pru, are you okay?"

Pru. Which made her Kennedy's eldest sister.

Christ. He needed to get ahold of himself. Flynn relaxed his grip and leaned back. Seeming to collect herself, Pru shifted from his lap—more was the pity—and reached up to take the offered hand. That was when he realized the owner of the hand was a young girl.

"I'm fine. The ladder tipped."

The girl, who had to be Ari, looked down at him with bright, curious eyes. "Who'd you land on?"

Flynn rolled to his feet, offering his hand, as more people came into the barn, including the familiar face he'd come looking for.

"Flynn Bohannon!"

He grinned and opened his arms wide. When Kennedy leapt into them, he swung her in a circle. "It's good to see you, *deifiúr beag.*"

"Back atcha, boy-o! We weren't expecting you until tomorrow."

"I thought I'd surprise you. But I seem to have interrupted some sort of festivities. Are you getting ready for a party, then?"

"Oh, yeah, about that. There's someone I want you to meet." Kennedy pulled back and held her hand out to a broad-shouldered man, with close-cropped brown hair and a steady gaze. He slid his arm around her shoulders, and she looked up at him with absolute adoration. "Xander, this is my brother from another mother, Flynn. Flynn, Xander Kincaid, my fiancé."

Flynn's mouth fell open. "Your what now?"

Kennedy laughed. "It's our wedding we're decorating for. We're getting married on Saturday."

"Married?" Flynn repeated. Was she insane? She'd been home, what, four months? If that.

She laughed again, fairly glowing with happiness. "It's a long story, and I'll tell you all about it over a pint later. First, I want you to meet my family. This is Ari." She laid her hands on the shoulders of the young Hispanic girl, with the dark, soulful eyes and ready grin.

"Pleased to meet you," Flynn said, shaking her hand.

"And this is Pru."

"We've met," they said in unison.

Kennedy arched her brows.

"She fell out of the sky," Flynn said.

"More properly, I fell off a ladder," Pru corrected. "Thanks for saving me from breaking my neck."

He mimed doffing a hat and bowed. "Happy to be of service, milady. Perhaps you'll let someone taller assist you in finishing with the lights?"

Pru flushed. "Oh, you're a guest. I'm not—oh my God, your room's not ready." She looked, if possible, even more flustered by that than she had crashing into him.

She was already turning toward the door, when Flynn caught her hand. "It's fine. Don't trouble on my account. I arrived early and unannounced. Just shove me in a closet or something. I'll be fine." That sent his mind off on a merry little jaunt, imagining what it would be like to drag Pru into a linen closet and get to know the rest of those lovely curves.

She looked scandalized, and he wondered if he'd said that aloud. Or maybe it was that he'd been rubbing circles on the back of her hand with his thumb.

"You're a guest at our inn. You'll have a proper room. Just give me fifteen minutes—twenty at the outside."

"Psh," Kennedy snorted. "He's family."

"The family all have beds," Pru argued.

Now was definitely *not* the time to suggest sharing hers. And really, he needed to quash this whole reaction. This was Kennedy's *sister*.

"Fine. You fix a room. *I'm* putting him to work. He and Xander can finish with the lights. Maggie and Athena should be back from their fitting soon, and it's Athena's turn to cook dinner."

Pru tugged her hand free and started for the door. "Fifteen minutes," she repeated. "Ari, come help me please."

Because he wanted to watch her go, Flynn deliberately turned toward the ladder and righted it. "Right. Lights?"

"To start." Kennedy grinned.

He propped an arm on one of the rungs and gave her the side eye. "Oh, so that's how it is? You're going to make me work for my supper?"

"I'm going to make you play for it. I want you to play for the wedding. Will you? I know it's last minute and all, but you're here and there's no one else I'd rather hear."

Flynn still wanted to know the story behind this sudden rush to the altar. But given her fiancé was watching him from ten feet away, he opted for the only safe answer. "I'd be honored."

Kennedy threw her arms around him in another, staggering hug. "Oh, thank you!"

"Anything for you. Now, where are the rest of these lights?"

Get your copy today!

What I Like About You
Rescue My Heart #2

A horse-whispering loner

After years as an Army Ranger, Sebastian Donnelly is content to be left alone with his horses. He's better with them than with...people. But that changes when his boss's little sister shows up. There's something about her, a vulnerability that tugs at his need to rescue. And a sexy, vivacious charm that ignites an attraction he ought to ignore.

A soon-to-be lawyer

Desperate for a break before her last semester of law school, Laurel Maxwell is excited to see her brother marry the woman he loves. Logan and Athena, their happiness, the life they're building at the farm all serve as a reminder that she's barreling toward a future she's no longer sure she wants. One her overbearing father insists is the only path she's meant for.

Who's rescuing who?

When Laurel is offered the chance to stay on the farm and dogsit while the happy couple honeymoons, she jumps at the chance to get out her life and into Sebastian's strong arms. He wants to help her make her decision, a choice with haunting echoes of his own past. But is there any path that leads to a forever where a brilliant lawyer and reclusive horse trainer could build a life together?

* * *

Chapter One

Sebastian Donnelly shifted in the saddle, giving the chestnut mare a subtle nudge with his knee. After only a moment's hesitation, Gingersnap switched directions, resuming her trot around the training ring.

"There's a girl."

Her ears swiveled back toward the sound of his crooning voice, so he kept up a low patter of one-sided conversation as they continued to circle. She was attentive to every touch, every signal, every shift of his weight, and it was immensely satisfying that she did it out of a desire to please him rather than out of fear.

She'd come a long way in the eight months since she'd been rescued. No one looking at her now would know she'd spent the last few years of her life subjected to profound neglect and abuse. She'd put on weight, so her ribs no longer showed through. The coat that had been dull and matted on her arrival now shone with a gleam. The mane and tail he'd spent weeks detangling, as he slowly, methodically earned her trust, fluttered with the breeze of her movement. He'd waited months before going near her with a saddle and bridle, and longer still before trying to ride her. She hadn't been ready. But over the past few weeks, it had become clear that she'd had training before landing with the asshole who'd let her damn near starve to death. The sweet temperament he'd seen beneath the fear had emerged like daffodils in the spring, and Sebastian marveled that her spirit hadn't been fully broken.

This was the joy and the miracle of the work he did. The work that had saved his own broken spirit.

A flash of movement at the rail caused a hitch in

Ginger's gait. Sebastian saw his stable girl climbing up so she could see better.

"She's looking fantastic!" At fifteen, Ari was bright, eager, and utterly besotted with all things equine. She'd been trading stable labor for additional riding lessons since the spring, so she was a familiar part of Sebastian's day.

"Coming along," he agreed, slowing the mare to a walk.

"Can I ride her?"

Sebastian shot her a look. All of his rescues had an assortment of behavioral issues he'd been working on since they came to the farm, and many weren't part of the group he used for lessons.

Ari folded her hands and put on her begging face. "Please? Just for a few minutes? I could stay on the lunge line."

He considered it. She'd proven herself a capable rider, quick to take instruction or correction, and Ginger was turning out to be a gentle, responsive mount. It might be a good fit.

Even as he thought it, the mare tensed beneath him and began to dance. Her ears twitched in agitation. Then he heard what she had.

Thunder.

It rolled over the land, echoing off the mountains that cupped this little pocket of paradise. As Ginger gave a little buck and twist, sidestepping across the ring, Sebastian ignored Ari, switching his full attention to his mount.

"Easy. Easy. Settle."

Tension crackled around her as he brought her in line. She quivered beneath him, nostrils flaring as he held her through another rumble of thunder. Her war between an instinct to flee and a desire to please him was evident in the way she tossed her head, eyes rolling. Storms were a huge trigger for her, and the only way to overcome that trigger was to keep pulling it, making her face it. Given their exceptionally dry autumn, there'd been limited opportunity to work on it, so he had to take the chances as they came.

For another twenty minutes, he battled her fear, taking the mare through her paces, despite the incoming storm. Ginger's anxiety was a palpable thing, and Sebastian deliberately banked his own emotions, knowing she'd ultimately mirror him. He just had to remind her of that trust. When she hesitated, he coaxed her through. When she danced, he reminded her to follow his lead. And when the first fat drops of rain began to splatter, he relented, reining her in long enough to dismount. Stepping close, he laid a hand on her quivering neck. "It's all right. You're all right."

Ginger held for him, though it was clear in every tense muscle that she still wanted to bolt.

Stripping the saddle as quickly as possible, he heaved it over a rail and led her to the adjacent pasture. There, he removed the bridle and set her loose. As the next boom of thunder rolled, the mare took off at a run, kicking up her back legs and galloping a wide circle of the pasture as the other horses looked on. A few were already plodding toward the three-walled shelter to get out of the rain.

Ari came to join him, hood up and hands shoved into the pockets of her coat against the cold December wind. "Think she'll ever get over her fear of storms?"

"Maybe someday. She's got a long way to go." He didn't know what had happened to the mare to instill this abject panic, but he'd learned early on that keeping her in the barn was a non-starter. It was a damned miracle she hadn't broken a leg in her terror the one time he'd tried. All in all, the entire herd did better when they weren't confined.

Sebastian and Ari both stared after Ginger for another couple of minutes, waiting until she'd run off her first burst of anxiety. He couldn't stop the worry or the guilt the niggled. Had he done enough? Should she be further along? It was fruitless speculation. The mare was where she was. There were only so many hours in the day, and the reality was that many of his were tied up with the riding school. It was a necessary evil—one he hoped would eventually make his rescue program self-sustaining. But that was a long way off. For now, that meant more time with students and less time one-on-one with his rescues. Slower progress was still progress.

"Help you clean up?" Ari asked.

"Appreciate it." Sebastian hefted the saddle, while she grabbed the bridle, and they made their way to the barn. "You got a ride home?"

"Logan's taking me. Are you sure it's not a problem I won't be around for the next few days?"

Her earnestness amused him. "It's not every day your aunt gets married. It's fine. Logan's bringing in some extra help for dealing with the rest of the stock while he and Athena are away."

The man himself showed up as they were stowing gear in the tack room. "Looks like we're in for a gullywasher."

"Yep," Sebastian agreed. "Worst ought to be done before too late tonight, though."

Logan slung an arm around his soon-to-be niece. "You about finished, kiddo?"

"I need to grab my backpack from the house."

He jerked his head. "Go on and do that. I wanna try to get you home before the storm breaks."

When he continued to linger after Ari had run off, Sebastian knew he had something on his mind.

"Something up?"

"Well, I actually wanted to ask a favor."

"Is there something else you needed me to take care of, while you and Athena are gone on your honeymoon?"

"What? Oh, no. It's about the wedding itself. My college friend Nick is one of my groomsmen, and he's not gonna be able to make it. His dad just had a heart attack this morning."

"That's terrible." *What does that have to do with me?*

"Yeah. It's looking like he's gonna be okay, but Nick doesn't want to leave him, and anyway it puts us one man short on my side. I was hoping you'd be willing to be a stand-in groomsman."

Sebastian blinked. "You want me to be in your wedding?

Logan's mouth quirked up in a grin. "I know it's last minute and there's a monkey suit and all that. But I consider you a friend and it happens you're about Nick's build."

Sebastian wasn't exactly keen on getting up in the middle of all the wedding festivities. There was a reason he worked with horses instead of people. Still, he owed Logan a lot.

The man had taken on a handful of horses simply because there'd been a need and he'd had the space. With his hands already full from managing all the moving parts of his organic farm, he'd needed help. As a favor to their mutual friend, Porter, Logan had turned over the care of the horses to Sebastian, giving him a job, a home, and a new purpose—something that had been sorely lacking since he'd separated from the military. He'd fully supported Sebastian's expanded equine rescue efforts, going so far as to delegate a solid chunk of acreage and the original barn at Maxwell Farms to that purpose. Over the past eleven months, and through the joint labor of fully restoring that barn to be a working stable, he'd become a friend. He'd stood for Sebastian through some seriously dark days, and Sebastian was humbled to be asked to stand up with him on one of his brightest.

"I'd be honored, man."

He blew out a relieved breath. "You're saving my ass."

"Athena doesn't strike me as the type to give a shit whether the numbers are even or whatever." The award-winning chef would probably only care about the food, so long as they were married by the end of the day.

"She's not. My mama is. None of us want to deal with her fretting about what Emily Post etiquette thing isn't being met."

Clearly, Logan fell a very long way from that particular family tree.

"What do you need me to do?"

"The rehearsal is tomorrow at 4:30 up at the Methodist church. After that, we'll all be headed back to the inn for the rehearsal dinner. I'll see that you get the tux when you get there. Then it's just showing up at one on Saturday to do pictures before the ceremony and hanging out through the wedding and the reception after. Once the final group pictures are taken, you're free to bail."

"I'd planned to be at the wedding and reception anyway." He was a sucker for wedding cake, and rumor had it that Athena's pastry chef from her former Chicago restaurant was making it.

"Great. I really appreciate it, man." Logan offered his hand.

"No problem. Guess I'll be seeing you at 4:30 tomorrow."

As Logan headed up to the house to grab Ari and take her home, Sebastian rubbed a hand over his beard, noting it had gotten kind of scraggly. His horses didn't give a shit what he looked like, but he still had enough of his mama's voice in his head telling him what was right and proper. Looked like he'd need to clean up like civilized folks.

* * *

Laurel was so late.

She had reasonable faith that her big brother

wouldn't excommunicate her from the wedding party and, from what she could tell, neither would his bride-to-be. But she knew perfectly well her mother would be having a hissy fit right about now, and nobody wanted to deal with that.

She'd been all set to get out the door of her Nashville apartment on time for the four-hour drive. But then The Call had come. The official job offer from Carson, Danvers, Herbert, and Pike up in New York. Roger Pike had called her himself to say how excited they all were to have her—as if it was a foregone conclusion that she'd accept the job, pending her upcoming graduation and the passing of the bar exam. It should have been. Newly-minted attorneys were not supposed to turn down offers from a top-five firm in the nation. Especially one with a starting salary like the one Pike had thrown at her. It had taken all of Laurel's considerable skill with words to navigate the conversation without giving an actual answer. Then another loss of precious time to come down from the post-call spaz so she was safe to drive.

She'd already been wound up about seeing her parents this weekend without having the spectre of this job hanging over the proceedings. She couldn't tell them. Wouldn't, even if she'd accepted. This weekend was about Logan and Athena, not her latest effort to please her father. But with every mile into the mountains, her shoulders tightened and her stomach churned.

What if Pike had told Dad himself? They'd clerked together once upon a time, long before Laurel's father had opened his own firm. She didn't think the job had been a result of nepotism—her class ranking at Vanderbilt spoke for itself. But she knew connections mattered. And she knew if she said no, the shock waves would have far-reaching repercussions. So, priority one was keeping the news under wraps so Logan and Athena had a drama-free wedding. If Dad already knew about the offer—well, she'd find a way to talk him down so it didn't turn the weekend into a shit show.

In the end, she pulled into the lot of the First Methodist Church, in tiny Eden's Ridge, Tennessee, a whopping forty-five minutes late. Whipping her Mini Cooper into a space, Laurel took a few seconds to run a brush through her hair and thumb two antacids off the roll in her purse before sprinting in her sensible heels to the front doors. In the vestibule, she paused to bring her breathing under control. Rosalind Maxwell would consider gasping for breath an unseemly insult to Laurel's already unforgivable tardiness.

Beyond the double doors leading into the sanctuary, she could hear the murmur of voices. Crap, they were probably wrapping up already. It wasn't like it took that long to practice walking down the aisle. When she thought she could speak without wheezing—really, she needed to carve out time to get back into the gym next semester—Laurel stepped inside. The voices stopped and all eyes turned to her. She resisted the urge to hunch her shoulders, instead pausing in the doorway, spine straight, shoulders back, all her debutante training coming to her aid.

If you're going to make an entrance, make an entrance.

"I'm so sorry I'm late. There was a pile-up on the I-40 on my way out of town." The lie rolled easily off her tongue. Traffic accidents fell under the heading of excuses her parents would accept. She could see them twisted around in a pew up front. Ignoring the moue of disappointment pinching her mother's pretty face, Laurel deliberately blanked her expression and strode down the red-carpeted aisle toward the assembled wedding party.

Grinning, Logan broke free of his position at the altar, long legs eating up the last several feet, so he could wrap her in a solid hug. "Good to see you, Pip."

She didn't bother rolling her eyes at the old nickname—short for Pipsqueak. Even in her heels, her brother towered over her. Instead, she burrowed in for a long moment, absorbing his natural calm. "Back atcha, big brother."

Hooking his arm around her shoulders, he led her the rest of the way to the front. "Everybody, I want y'all to meet my sister, Laurel."

She gave a little wave. As Logan began introductions to the rest of the wedding party, she was aware of her parents' disapproving glares.

"—remember Athena, and these are her sisters, Maggie, Kennedy, and Pru. And this young lady with the sappy, romantic grin is Pru's daughter Ari. She likes to matchmake. Consider yourself warned."

Ari snorted. "Whatever. You're here, aren't you? That's a three-for-three success rate."

"I'm not sure you can claim credit for all of those," Kennedy pointed out.

The girl crossed her arms. "Who was it who gave you all a stern talking to when you were being idiots?"

Pru shot her daughter a look of affectionate reproof. "What she means is she's an incurably nosy and interfering romantic."

"I regret nothing," the teenager insisted.

Logan ruffled her hair. "Noted, Nosy. Moving on. This is our wedding planner, Cayla Black; my friend, Porter Ingram; and you remember Xander."

Did she ever. Her brother's former college

roommate was still hot. He was also very married. To Kennedy, if she wasn't mistaken. They'd been high school sweethearts, once upon a time, and life had given them a second chance.

"Good to see you again, Xander. Congrats on your own nuptials."

He wrapped her a quick hug. "Thanks. You grew up."

"Yeah, that happens. I'm all set to become a productive member of society and everything."

"So I hear. Never pegged you for law school as a kid."

Laurel's face felt stiff as she forced it into a smile. "It takes all kinds."

Logan continued with the introductions. "And this is Pru's husband, Flynn."

Flynn nodded with an expression every bit as impish as his daughter's. "A pleasure, to be sure." The greeting fell off his tongue with an unmistakable Irish brogue.

"This here is Master of Carbs, Athena's pal, Moses Lindsey. Moses is the genius behind our cake."

"I'm pretty sure that makes you the most popular guy at the wedding," Laurel told him.

His teeth flashed white against the burnished bronze of his face. "I aim to please."

"Please tell me there's chocolate." She folded her hands in supplication.

Moses jerked his head in Ari's direction. "Tiny over there already put in her order. There will be chocolate," he confirmed.

Laurel mimed a small fist pump. "You are a god among men." Chocolate cake would go a long way toward making up for the stress she'd endured this semester.

"And last but certainly not least, your escort, Sebastian Donnelly."

Laurel turned to the last groomsman and felt the faux, flirty smile slide right off her face. She froze there, hand partly outstretched as her gaze locked with a pair of deep, brown eyes. Her breath backed up in her lungs, and her heart slowed to a crawl.

His thick, dark hair was nearly black and just a little mussed, as if he'd combed it with his fingers straight from the shower. Broad shoulders tapered to a narrow waist and long, long legs. His button-down shirt clung to his arms in a way that told her he had plenty of muscle under the Oxford cloth, and she'd bet money there was a solid six-pack under there, too.

He stepped forward, taking her hand in his. "Hi."

As his long, callused fingers closed around hers,

she could breathe again. A stillness seemed to flow out of him and into her, and all the running and the stressing and the anxiety that was her constant companion went quiet. Her breath came out on something very close to a sigh, the tension in her shoulders leeching out. In its absence, the pulse that had turned sluggish began to gallop. All the prospective polite banter evaporated from her brain, leaving her with only one thought: *Holy shit, you're gorgeous.*

She couldn't very well say that, though.

Words. I need words. I'm supposed to be good at those. Casting around for something to say, she blurted, "What happened to Nick?" Goofy, bespectacled Nick, who used to give her noogies and didn't leave her a tongue-tied mess of attraction.

"His dad had a heart attack, so Sebastian is standing-in," Logan explained.

"Is his dad okay?" The question came automatically. Thank God, she sounded normal at least.

"Yeah, he came through surgery and woke up a few hours ago."

"Good," she murmured.

Sebastian still had her hand, still hadn't looked away. Why hadn't he moved? Why hadn't she? It seemed as if heat built between their palms, and Laurel wanted to bask in it.

She wasn't broken. After the last couple of

years, she'd begun to think that Devon had been right. The last guy she'd tried dating, back in her first year of law school, he'd accused her of being a robot. She was driven and focused. In the grand scheme of trying to maintain her position at the top of her class through that brutal, first year of academic hazing, dating and sex hadn't been a priority. She hadn't been interested in anyone since. But standing here, palm-to-palm, with Sebastian Donnelly, she felt that interest roar to life like a furnace re-stoked. Heat rolled over her, and she could only pray she wasn't blushing.

One corner of his mouth quirked, as if he knew her brain wasn't firing on all cylinders. Christ, how was it legal for a man to have lips that sensual? The contrast to the neat, close-cropped beard did something to her long-dormant lady parts, and she couldn't help wondering what that beard would feel like on the sensitive skin of her inner thighs.

"—done with introductions, how about we do one last run through, so Laurel is up-to-speed, then we'll break for the rehearsal dinner. Okay?"

Jerking her attention to Cayla, Laurel pulled her hand free, resisting the urge to tuck it under her arm to savor the tingles from where he'd touched it. Her cheeks bloomed with warmth.

Good God, when was the last time she'd felt an attraction like this?

Pretty sure that would be never, she thought as she followed the other bridesmaids to the vestibule.

With half an ear, Laurel listened to the wedding planner reel off instructions. The rest of her was still back in the sanctuary, reliving the touch of Sebastian's hand. It wasn't the heat that drew her—though that had rocked her back plenty—it was the stillness. The same kind of calmness her brother had always exuded but...more, somehow. Rare and precious, that feeling called her more effectively than any siren. Taking her place in the line-up to walk down the aisle, she wondered what she had to do to get another hit.

Grab your copy of *What I Like About You* today!

Other Books By Kait Nolan

A complete and up-to-date list of all my books can be found at https:// kaitnolan.com.

Gibson Hollow
Small Town Southern Romance

- Hero After Midnight (prequel)
- Hero Ever After (Alia and Ramsey)
- Hero, Unexpected (Bodie and Emmaline)

Kilted Hearts
Small Town Contemporary Scottish Romance

- *Jilting The Kilt* (prequel)
- *Cowboy in a Kilt* (Raleigh and Kyla)
- *Grump in a Kilt* (Malcolm and Charlotte)
- *Playboy in a Kilt* (Connor and Sophie)
- *Protector in a Kilt* (Ewan and Isobel)
- *Single Dad in a Kilt* (Hamish and Afton)
- *Kilty Pleasures* (Jason and Skye)

SPECIAL OPS SCOTS
SMALL TOWN MILITARY SCOTTISH ROMANCE

- *One Fine Night* (prequel)
- *Before Highland Sunset* (Alex and Ciara)
- *Beyond Highland Sunrise* (Callum and Parker)
- *Beneath Highland Stars* (Finley and Saoirse)

BAD BOY BAKERS
SMALL TOWN MILITARY ROMANCE

- *Rescued By a Bad Boy* (Brax and Mia prequel)
- *Mixed Up With a Marine* (Brax and Mia)

- *Wrapped Up with a Ranger* (Holt and Cayla)
- *Stirred Up by a SEAL* (Jonah and Rachel)
- *Hung Up on the Hacker* (Cash and Hadley)
- *Caught Up with the Captain* (Grey and Rebecca)

RESCUE MY HEART SERIES
SMALL TOWN MILITARY ROMANCE

- *Someone Like You* (Ivy and Harrison)
- *What I Like About You* (Laurel and Sebastian)
- *Bad Case of Loving You* (Paisley and Ty prequel) Included in *Made For Loving You* (Paisley and Ty)

THE MISFIT INN SERIES
SMALL TOWN FAMILY ROMANCE

- *When You Got A Good Thing* (Kennedy and Xander)
- *Til There Was You* (Misty and Denver)
- *Those Sweet Words* (Pru and Flynn)
- *Stay A Little Longer* (Athena and Logan)

- *Bring It On Home* (Maggie and Porter)
- *Come Away with Me* (Moses and Zuri)

MEN OF THE MISFIT INN
SMALL TOWN SOUTHERN ROMANCE

- *Let It Be Me* (Emerson and Caleb)
- *Our Kind of Love* (Abbey and Kyle)
- *Don't You Wanna Stay* (Deanna and Wyatt)
- *Until We Meet Again* (Samantha and Griffin prequel)
- *Come A Little Closer* (Samantha and Griffin)
- *Just Wanted You To Know* (Livia and Declan)
- *A Love Like You* (Juliette and Mick)

WISHFUL ROMANCE SERIES
SMALL TOWN SOUTHERN ROMANCE

- *To Get Me To You* (Cam and Norah)
- *Know Me Well* (Liam and Riley)
- *Be Careful, It's My Heart* (Brody and Tyler)
- *The Matchmaker Maneuver* (Myles and Piper prequel)

- *Just For This Moment* (Myles and Piper)
- *Wish I Might* (Reed and Cecily)
- *Turn My World Around* (Tucker and Corinne)
- *Dance Me A Dream* (Jace and Tara)
- *See You Again* (Trey and Sandy)
- *The Christmas Fountain* (Chad and Mary Alice)
- *You Were Meant For Me* (Mitch and Tess)
- *A Lot Like Christmas* (Ryan and Hannah)
- *Dancing Away With My Heart* (Zach and Lexi)

WISHFUL MOMENTS SERIES
BITE-SIZED WISHFUL ROMANCE

- *Once Upon A Coffee* (Avery and Dillon)
- *Once Upon A Rescue* (Brooke and Hayden)
- *Who I Am with You* (Dinah and Robert)

WISHING FOR A HERO SERIES (A WISHFUL SPINOFF SERIES)

SMALL TOWN ROMANTIC SUSPENSE

- *Make You Feel My Love* (Judd and Autumn)
- *Watch Over Me* (Nash and Rowan)
- *Can't Take My Eyes Off You* (Ethan and Miranda)
- *Burn For You* (Sean and Delaney)

MEET CUTE ROMANCE
SMALL TOWN SHORT ROMANCE

- *Once Upon A Snow Day*
- *Once Upon A New Year's Eve*
- *Once Upon An Heirloom*

SUMMER FLING TRILOGY
CONTEMPORARY ROMANCE

- *Second Chance Summer*
- *Summer Camp Secret*
- *The Summer Camp Swap*

About Kait

Kait is a Mississippi native, who often swears like a sailor, calls everyone sugar, honey, or darlin', and can wield a bless your heart like a saber or a Snuggie, depending on requirements.

You can find more information on this *USA Today* best selling and RITA ® Award-winning author and her books on her website http://kaitnolan.com.

Do you need more small town sass and spark? Sign up for <u>her newsletter</u> to hear about new releases, book deals, and exclusive content!

www.ingramcontent.com/pod-product-compliance
Lightning Source LLC
Chambersburg PA
CBHW071520100726
47908CB00004B/1234